The Mystery
of the Silver Star

The Silver Star stood gleaming and proud. Willoughby circled it, motioning for everyone but Frank to stand away.

"It really is a marvelous piece of work, isn't it?" Willoughby said.

"You haven't seen anything yet," Frank said, preparing to mount the bike.

"Now!" shouted Joe.

Everything happened at once. Frank hopped on the Silver Star and began pedaling like crazy. Joe launched himself into the air, aiming his shoulder directly at Derek Willoughby's stomach. Keith leaped for the front door and opened it just in time for Frank to go sailing through on the bike.

"You fools!" Frank could hear Willoughby shouting, but his voice was already fading as Frank rode the Silver Star to freedom.

The Hardy Boys Mystery Stories

Available from MINSTREL Books

86

The HARDY BOYS®

THE MYSTERY OF THE SILVER STAR

FRANKLIN W. DIXON

A MINSTREL® BOOK

PUBLISHED BY POCKET BOOKS

New York   London   Toronto   Sydney   Tokyo   Singapore

A MINSTREL PAPERBACK *ORIGINAL*

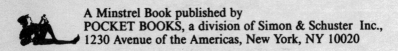

A Minstrel Book published by
POCKET BOOKS, a division of Simon & Schuster Inc.,
1230 Avenue of the Americas, New York, NY 10020

ISBN: 0-671-64374-6

Produced by Mega-Books of New York, Inc.

First Minstrel Books printing September 1987

10 9 8 7 6 5 4

THE HARDY BOYS MYSTERY STORIES, A MINSTREL BOOK and colophon are trademarks of Simon & Schuster Inc.

THE HARDY BOYS is a registered trademark of Simon & Schuster Inc.

Cover art by Paul Bachem

Printed in the U.S.A.

Contents

THE MYSTERY OF
THE SILVER STAR

1 Bike-Aid

"We're going to miss the race," Frank Hardy said to his brother, Joe.

"No we won't. There's a place—grab it!"

Frank quickly steered their van into a tight parking spot near the curb, and both boys jumped out.

At the edge of Bayport's town square, photographers, newspaper reporters, and TV news crews were already set up and waiting. In front of them, there was a banner hanging across Main Street. It read "Bayport Welcomes Bike-Aid Racers—Keith Holland and Gregg Angelotti!" A red, white, and blue stripe painted down the middle of Main Street marked the route leading to the town square.

"Do you believe how many kids are here on their bikes?" Joe said as he and his brother joined the crowd.

1

"Just keep your eyes open for trouble when Keith and Gregg arrive," Frank said.

Any minute now Bike-Aid would be arriving in Bayport, and that was big news. The town square was filled with people. Most of them had come to see America's two top cyclists, who had raced three thousand miles across the U.S. to raise money for the poor and homeless.

Or they had come to see the Silver Star—the high-tech bicycle built especially for Keith Holland to ride in this race.

Frank and Joe Hardy were there for another reason—they knew something was going wrong, terribly wrong, with the Bike-Aid race. Keith Holland was in trouble, and he needed their help.

Suddenly someone came out of Wilson's Ice Cream Shoppe and started yelling and waving at Frank and Joe. They turned around and saw their good friend Chet Morton pushing his way through the crowd. He was holding a double-scoop blueberry ice cream cone. When he reached Frank and Joe, Chet began speaking quickly into his ice cream cone as if it were a microphone.

"And here they are, ladies and gentlemen," Chet said, "Bayport's pride and joy, that duo of dynamite detective work, Frank and Joe Hardy! Let's see if I can get an interview with eighteen-year-old Frank Hardy, the brown-haired, brown-eyed older of the two—"

"Chet, your microphone is melting all over your arm," Joe interrupted.

Chet ignored Joe and pointed his double-dip microphone in Frank's direction. "Young man," he said in a deep voice, "give me your honest opinion. Don't you think all of this hoopla is a bit much for just a silver-colored bicycle?"

"Calling the Silver Star just a silver-colored bicycle," Frank said, "is like comparing you to Tony Prito. It's impossible!" Tony was another good friend of the Hardys. He was small, wiry, and fast. Chet, on the other hand, was tall and heavyset.

"Yeah, well, I'm built for endurance, not speed," Chet replied good-naturedly.

"The Silver Star was built for *both*," Frank said. "It has new gear ratios, new metals, a totally different frame geometry. Keith Holland is riding ten thousand dollars' worth of R and D."

"Listen to him—'R and D,'" Chet said.

"Research and development," Joe translated.

"Wow," Chet said, taking a large bite of his microphone. "This dude really knows what he's talking about."

"That's my brother," said Joe, pushing his mirrored sunglasses up on his nose.

"So what are you guys doing here?"

"Same as you—we came to see the Silver Star," Joe answered, running a hand through his blond hair.

3

"Wait a minute, you two," Chet said. Then he stared at his watch, pretending to wait a full sixty seconds before saying anything else. But Chet Morton could never go that long between sentences. "If you will check my birth certificate, you will see that I was not born yesterday. You can't fool me. I've known the two of you long enough to know that you're here on a case!"

Joe was curious, so he bit first. "What makes you think so?" he asked.

"Well, for one thing, when you're on a case, you always wear sunglasses so I can't see your blue eyes watching everything in sight," Chet said to Joe. "And for another, Frank always comes off like a walking encyclopedia on topics he didn't used to know anything about. So what's going on? Come on, you guys can trust me."

"Con Riley called us last night and said that Keith Holland is in some kind of trouble," Frank told Chet. "He said Keith wanted to talk to us when he arrived in Bayport. That's all we know."

"I don't get it. Why would Keith call Officer Riley?"

"Con Riley is an old friend of a friend of Keith's," Frank explained. "Keith called Con yesterday and said that someone has been trying to sabotage the race, trying to make sure that Keith doesn't finish."

Chet's eyes lit up, and he gave them his best "I've solved this case for you" smile. "Doesn't

4

the name Gregg Angelotti mean anything to you guys? I mean, talk about the perfect suspect for sabotage. Gregg Angelotti and Keith Holland have been major rivals for years!"

The name Gregg Angelotti meant many things to Frank and Joe Hardy. It meant corporate power, because Gregg was sponsored by Am-Bike, the largest bicycle manufacturing company in the U.S. The name Gregg Angelotti also meant maximum effort, minimum modesty, and total conceit. Biking magazines wrote one story after another about Gregg Angelotti's racing triumphs and off-the-course tantrums. He was the biker fans loved to hate. But fans and fellow racers alike had to respect Gregg for his talent.

"Here they come!" someone in the crowd shouted. Cameras and camcorders began spinning, and the excitement level in the crowd jumped one thousand percent.

Down Main Street came two young men wearing skin-tight brightly colored shirts and black bicycle pants. Black-haired Gregg Angelotti, on his red Am-Bike racer, had the lead. Blond, freckle-faced Keith Holland, on the gleaming Silver Star, trailed by about two hundred feet. They rode hunched over, heads down, bent double toward their handlebars.

"Look at their faces," Frank said, giving a low whistle of disbelief.

Keith and Gregg's faces were pale, almost white, showing the brutal effects of hours of exhaustion, dehydration, and pain.

The riders fell rather than climbed off their bikes. Trainers and crew hopped out of the caravan of trucks and campers that had been following the racers on the road. They pushed into the crowd to wrap blankets around Keith and Gregg. Then they helped the racers over to a flag-draped area in the town square for a quick press conference.

Frank and Joe noticed right away that Keith was limping.

"How do you feel?" a reporter asked him.

"I don't feel anything. My whole body is numb," Keith said, gasping for air. "But that's normal after such a long ride," he added with a smile. Standing next to Keith, Gregg drank a bottle of mineral water and ignored the reporters. That was vintage Angelotti style.

"Keith, how is the Silver Star performing?" asked a TV reporter.

"Beautifully! Just exactly as Michael Saperstein said it would." Keith smiled.

Keith never said a word about his bike without giving complete credit to the man who had designed and built the Silver Star. Unlike Am-Bike, Michael Saperstein was a one-man company, not a mega-corporation.

Saperstein was an ex-racer who had come up with a revolutionary new bike design, but he knew he could never compete with Am-Bike's enormous advertising budgets. Then he hit on the idea of starting Bike-Aid. By trying to raise money for the poor and homeless, Saperstein

6

realized he could also get a great deal of free publicity for the Silver Star.

Gregg Angelotti couldn't let talk of the Silver Star go by without a smart remark. "Yeah, the Silver Star is performing just as I expected," Gregg said. "S-L-O-W. And as long as Keith doesn't run out of Scotch tape, it may even finish the race!"

"Gregg," a woman reporter called out, "I've been following Bike-Aid, and the Silver Star looks pretty fast to me. Now, this isn't a real race, it's just a charity ride. But how do you think you're going to compete against the Silver Star in the Grand Prix tour next year?"

"That question is just as stupid today as it was yesterday!" Gregg snapped.

"Give them a break, Gregg, and answer their questions," Keith said. "They're just trying to do their job."

Gregg's exhausted face sprang to sudden life. "Hey! I don't tell you how to ride, and you don't tell me how to answer questions, got it?"

Just then, the mayor of Bayport stepped in to smooth things over with some well-chosen words and two keys to the city. Then the racers posed for photos, shook hands, and signed autographs while local clubs presented them with checks made out to Bike-Aid. Finally, Greg and Keith decided that it was time to head for their campers.

"Let's go!" Frank said to his brother, and they quickly followed along. Chet had gone back

7

earlier for another double-dip ice cream cone, so he was left behind.

The campers—where the racers would sleep for the night before continuing on to New York City, Boston, and their final destination in Maine—were parked temporarily on a side street a few blocks from the town square. Soon they would be moved to a local trailer park. There was one for Keith and one for Gregg. Gregg's said Am-Bike on it in big, bold letters. There were also a few extra campers, which Frank and Joe figured were for support crews and Am-Bike representatives.

As the Hardys rounded the corner, they saw Keith disappear into a beige camper at the end of the block. Standing outside the camper was a burly man in his sixties with red hair and a ruddy complexion. With his arms crossed, he looked more like a tree planted to block the door than a man standing in front of it.

"Hello, lads," he said as Frank and Joe came near.

"We'd like to see Keith Holland," Joe said.

"I'm sure you would, lads," said the man, with a trace of an Irish brogue. "But I'm afraid he's resting now. I know exactly what you want, though." The man reached into a manila envelope he carried and handed Frank an autographed photo of Keith Holland.

"No, *you* don't get the picture," Frank said. "Keith wants to see *us*."

"Oh, I'm sure Keith would see all of his fans if it were up to him. But, lads, I'd be betraying my duty as his trainer if I didn't make sure that he gets all the rest he needs. So go home, boys." Frank started to speak, but the huge man bellowed at him, "Those are my final words!" Then he went into the camper and locked the door.

"Well, I guess that's that," Frank said to Joe. "If Keith Holland wants to see us, his trainer doesn't seem to know or care anything about it."

"Maybe, maybe not," Joe said. "But let's leave him a note, just in case." Joe took the photo of Keith from his brother and wrote their names and telephone number on the back. Then he stuffed it into the handle of the camper door.

To make up for their case not getting off the ground yet, Frank and Joe decided to treat themselves to double bacon cheeseburgers at the Bayport Diner. Then they took in a double feature, followed by a late-night game of one-on-one basketball in the courtyard outside their old elementary school. It was midnight before they finally got home.

Their mother, Laura Hardy, was waiting for them in the kitchen when they came in.

"The phone's been ringing every twenty minutes," she said, and instantly the phone started to ring again.

"Who was it?" Frank asked his mom before picking up the receiver.

"Keith Holland. He sounded very upset."

9

"Hello?" Frank said into the phone. "This is Frank Hardy."

"Finally," said the voice on the other end. "This is Keith Holland. Could you come over to the Jackson Beach Trailer Park right away? Someone just tried to break into my camper!"

2 Keith Holland's Story

The Hardy brothers hopped into their dark blue police van, which had been given to them after the *Desert Phantom* case by Police Chief Collig, and headed out toward Jackson Beach. Finally, someone was going to fill in the details that Con Riley had left out. What was going on behind the scenes of Bike-Aid? What kind of trouble was Keith Holland in?

The Jackson Beach Trailer Park was a huge gravel lot on the far side of the highway across from the bay. Row upon row of mobile homes, trailers, campers, and RVs were lined up, each with its own individual water and electricity hookup. Even though it was after midnight, lights blazed from many of the vehicles, and Frank and Joe could hear the sounds of portable TVs from almost every one.

Driving through the entrance at the south end

of the park, Frank and Joe could see Gregg Angelotti's Winnebago and the others that carried his support crew and the Am-Bike people. But Keith Holland had instructed Frank to come to the north end of the park. There they found Keith's beige camper.

They knocked on the door and were greeted by Keith's red-haired trainer, the burly man who had chased them away earlier.

"Well, lads," he said gaily, stepping out of the camper, "my name's P.J. O'Malley. I guess I was wrong about you this afternoon. My apologies."

Before Frank or Joe could say anything, the man dropped his voice so that Keith, inside the camper, couldn't hear him. "Keep him calmed down, lads," he said. "Tell him anything he wants to hear. He'll never be able to race with this on his mind."

"It's just a race for charity," Joe said. "You make it sound like a matter of life and death."

"Don't kid yourself," P.J. said. Then he walked out, leaving the doorway clear for Frank and Joe to enter the camper.

Keith's brightly lit camper was packed to overflowing with audio- and video-cassettes, TV and VCR, stereo, health-food jars and wrappers, clothes, trophies and prize ribbons, exercise equipment, books, the world's largest collection of photos and posters of circus bears on bicycles, vitamin jars, and newspapers and magazines.

Hanging from the ceiling, off in a corner, was the fabulous shining metal bike, the Silver Star.

12

It was on display like a work of art, which made sense to Frank. To him it *was* a work of art.

Keith Holland lay tilted back on a slant board with electric heating pads wrapped around his blue-jeaned legs to keep his muscles warm and loose. He removed the pads and stood up when he saw the Hardys, greeting them with a friendly smile.

"Boy, am I glad to finally meet you guys," Keith said. "Someone tried to break in here tonight—while I was sleeping!"

"You'd better start at the beginning, by telling us what's going on," Frank said. "Con Riley didn't really give us any details. He just said you think someone is trying to sabotage your race."

"Right. It started about four days ago," Keith said, sitting down carefully. He put a cushion under his left knee. "It seemed like pranks at first. Like when someone put salt water in my water bottle. You know we carry water with us all the time."

"Because you sweat so much on the road," Frank chimed in to demonstrate his knowledge of cycling.

"Right. Well, I picked up my water from its strap on the bike frame and squirted about a *gallon* of salt water into my mouth. I could have stopped riding and gotten fresh water from P.J., but I didn't want to give Gregg the satisfaction of going ahead. So I stuck with it and nearly went into shock from dehydration. It was stupid of me.

13

"Then, a couple of days later," Keith continued, "someone put some kind of incredible glue on my handlebars. I grabbed them and couldn't get free."

"You were wearing gloves, weren't you?" Frank asked.

Keith nodded. "Yeah, and it was a good thing I was, too! But that pair was ruined. The glue was so powerful, P.J. had to cut the gloves off the handlebars. Then we had to completely clean and retape my grips."

Finally, Keith handed Frank and Joe a copy of a newspaper from a city the racers had stopped in a week ago.

The headline read, "Biker Makes a Stop That's the Pits." It was a story about someone in town seeing Keith coming out of a bar very late at night.

"It's a total lie," Keith said.

"So far these things sound like—well, as you said—pranks," Joe commented. "And none of them sounds like a real crime. I'm not sure what we can do."

"Two nights ago," Keith went on, "when I came back to my camper, someone was standing on the steps, right up against the door. I knew immediately he was trying to break in. I yelled and charged at him, but he ducked around the camper faster than I've ever seen anyone move."

"Did you get a look at him?" Frank asked.

"It was too dark," Keith said. "Before I knew it, I felt a sharp pain in my neck. I guess he came

14

around the other side and hit me. I fell and twisted my knee a little when I hit the ground. He ran off, and I didn't chase him."

"So that's why you were limping today," Frank said.

"Yes. Don't tell P.J. this, but my knee has really been hurting. I've been babying it, but it could make a real difference in the race."

"And what happened tonight?" asked Joe.

"P.J. was out. I was here sound asleep," Keith said. "And I'll tell you, riding a bike for a hundred and fifty miles a day, twenty days in a row, brings new meaning to the words *sound asleep*."

"You've never heard our friend Chet Morton snore," Frank couldn't resist adding, and both brothers grinned.

"Usually nothing wakes me until P.J. gets me up in the morning," Keith said. "But something sure woke me up tonight. I felt the whole camper shake! And I heard someone trying to break in again. I ran to the door, unlocked it, and kicked it open."

"Ooh." Joe winced, turning his head away. He was imagining the kicked door smashing someone in the face.

"I didn't hit anyone," Keith said, smiling at Joe. "He was already off the steps." Keith opened the door to the camper and pointed off to the right. "It was too dark to see, but I definitely *heard* footsteps sprinting for the woods in that direction."

15

"Did you call the police?"

"Sure—Con Riley was up here. He said he'd investigate the attempted break-in. But, as he said, his jurisdiction is Bayport, not the whole U.S. This stuff has been happening to me on the road, and Con can't come along on the tour. That's why he suggested I contact you."

Frank nodded thoughtfully. "Let's take a look around, Joe," he said.

Each brother carried a halogen flashlight as they walked around Keith's camper. If they were lucky, they'd find something out of place, something dropped by the would-be burglar. But they had to settle for an interesting set of footprints.

When the Hardy brothers returned, Keith said, "P.J. thinks it was all a bad dream."

"We know you weren't dreaming," Frank said. "I checked your door on the way in. Someone was definitely tampering with the lock. We also found footprints leading away from your camper with a four-foot span between the steps."

"What does that mean?" Keith asked.

"Someone was running," Joe said simply. "But we lost the trail."

"Why would someone want to break in here?" Frank asked, but all three young men answered the question by looking up at the Silver Star hanging overhead.

"I can't believe anyone would want to steal the Silver Star," Keith said. "I mean, that

16

wouldn't make me give up the race. I have another bike."

"But you might lose the race," Joe pointed out.

"Any idea who might want that to happen?" asked Frank.

Keith didn't answer for a minute. Instead, he offered Frank and Joe bottles of mineral water from a half-sized refrigerator.

"I don't like to point fingers," Keith said finally, "but Gregg Angelotti is not a good loser, as everybody knows. And by now he knows what an incredible bike the Silver Star is. If I were him, I'd be nervous."

"Let me ask you something," Joe said slowly. "Is there any prize for this race? I mean, what would happen if you didn't finish the race? Does it matter who wins?"

"It always matters who wins," replied Keith. "A winner's competitive ranking and reputation are affected by every race."

Keith drained his bottle of water. Then he said, "No, there's no prize for winning this race. It's basically just a test of endurance. For every mile we ride, our sponsors kick in more money to Bike-Aid. So, if I drop out, or lose, Gregg will say that he raised more money for the homeless —and it'll be true. Maybe it's because I'm an orphan, but this fund-raiser really means a lot to me. It's just about pride, that's all. Pride."

Keith walked over to a large road map of the United States taped to the wall. A thick red line

17

stretched across the map like a snake, and the snake's head came to rest in Maine.

"Six more days. That's how long we figure it'll take us to finish the race. I'd really appreciate it if you'd come with me to Maine on the last leg of the tour. If I knew you were trying to find out who's sabotaging me, I'd forget about everything else except riding my race."

It was Frank and Joe's turn not to answer right away.

"Let's sleep on it and talk in the morning," Frank said.

"Okay," Keith said, shaking hands with the Hardys. "Come for breakfast around five in the morning."

"Five in the morning," Frank muttered as he and Joe walked back to their van. Then he turned to Joe. "Why didn't you say you'd take the case?"

"Why didn't you?"

"I asked you first."

Joe got behind the steering wheel of the van and started the engine. "Maybe we were thinking the same thing: Is Keith Holland telling the truth, or is he using us against his longtime rival? Gregg Angelotti is the natural suspect—everyone from Keith Holland to Chet Morton knows that. Maybe Keith thinks that Gregg will get nervous and lose the race if we start investigating, asking him questions."

"You're right," Frank said. "So the first ques-

18

tion we've got to answer is, do we think Keith Holland was lying to us?"

For a moment they thought again about Keith Holland's face and his voice and eyes—steady and direct.

"No, he's not lying," Joe said. "Something is really worrying him."

"I agree. Then let's go home and grab some sleep so we can get back here at five."

After Joe eased onto the road, he popped a cassette in the tape deck and said, "I think the situation calls for a little music."

They had driven to the south end of the camper park when a sudden loud noise from inside the van made both brothers tighten like mainsprings. *Scritch.* It was the sound of metal scraping against metal.

"What was that?" Joe shouted, trying not to take his eyes off the road to look behind.

Frank whirled around in the passenger seat.

There was a dark figure hiding in the back of the van. The intruder slid open the side door and lunged out!

3 Breakfast Meeting

Joe hit the brakes so hard his foot almost broke through the floorboard. But by the time he and Frank had unbuckled their seat belts, the intruder had jumped from the van and was running into the woods.

Frank leaped out of the van, shouting to Joe, "Turn around and give me the high beams!" Frank ran full speed into the woods, following the sounds of the fleeing stranger.

Tires squealed and kicked up dirt as Joe swung the van around. Then he, too, jumped out of the van and joined the chase on foot. But instead of following his brother, Joe made a wide circle around the woods that bordered the trailer park on two sides.

Through the trees, the Hardy brothers ran their separate, twisting paths. Frank was right behind the man who was running back toward the lights of the trailers. Joe hoped to cut off the unknown escaping sprinter from the front.

Suddenly Joe stopped and crouched behind a tree, breathing through his mouth as quietly as he could.

What a night, Joe thought to himself. Two bikers pedal into Bayport for a few hours, and suddenly we can't turn around without running into trouble!

Joe was a coiled spring, listening and waiting. Then he heard what he was waiting for—the thump, thump of running feet on a dirt path, coming closer to him. He leapt!

Joe was in midair, sailing like a missile for his target.

"Oomph!" his victim cried as Joe tackled him at the knees. They tumbled and rolled in the dirt, and Joe ended up on top.

"What were you doing in my van, creep!" Joe shouted to the man he was sitting on.

"I thought I was getting a ride home!" gasped his brother from flat on his back. "Get off me!"

Joe pounded the dirt with his fist. "What happened to the guy you were chasing?"

"I must have lost him at the crossroads," Frank said. "Come on, I'll show you where."

Frank and Joe ran back to a spot where three dirt paths converged. One path led to the trailer park's shower facilities, one led to the brightly lit trailer area, and one led deeper into the woods.

"If he ran back toward the park area, he could

21

have gone into any one of those campers," Frank said. "And there must be at least seventy-five of them here!"

Joe shook his head slowly. "It would take us all night to search the entire area. I don't know about you, but *I'm* not in the mood for a game of hide-and-go-seek in the dark."

"Maybe we should start by looking in *that* camper," Frank said, pointing to the camper where Gregg Angelotti was staying.

"We let this guy get away. That was bad enough. No use jumping to conclusions, too," Joe said, turning to go back to their van.

"Yeah, you've already *jumped* to enough conclusions for one night," Frank said, rubbing the bruised areas on his legs where his brother had tackled him.

"Next time, remember to wear white at night." Joe laughed.

Driving home, Frank played his usual mystery guessing game while Joe patiently listened to his brother think out loud. Frank had picked up the habit because of some advice his father had given him. Fenton Hardy, a former New York City police officer, was now a well-known private detective, and he had tried to teach his sons all the tricks of the trade.

"You start an investigation by driving yourself crazy with questions," Fenton Hardy had said. "Ask *yourself* questions first, then start asking other people. Eventually you'll ask the right question of the right person at the right time, and you'll start getting answers."

"Who was the man in the back of our van? What was he doing in here? Did he find what he was looking for?" Frank said out loud.

"I checked the van," Joe replied. "Nothing was stolen."

"Okay, did the guy think it was someone else's van, or did he know it belonged to us?" Frank went on. "Did he know we were on a case? Is this connected to the fact that someone tried to break into Keith Holland's camper tonight? Or is it a coincidence?"

The trouble with this guessing game—and what bugged Joe the most about it—was that there was no way to know any of the answers, not this early in the case. Answers would come slowly, maybe starting at five in the morning, when they met Keith Holland for breakfast.

Joe and Frank headed home for some sleep— about two hours of it, to be exact.

At four-thirty in the morning, the Hardy brothers were showered, dressed, and propelling themselves out their front door.

They drove to the trailer park, listening to their favorite cassette.

Even though it was still dark when they got to Keith's camper, breakfast was already in full swing. P.J. had loaded the small kitchen table with plates and bowls containing oatmeal, brown sugar, milk, toasted muffins, pancakes, grilled steak, fruit, juice, and vitamin supplements. But Keith wasn't eating much of it.

"P.J. likes to see me eat a huge breakfast," Keith said. "It's one thing he's old-fashioned about. But cyclists can't handle all this food on the road during the day. We do our carbo loading at night."

Frank and Joe had been waiting politely for Keith to offer them something to eat. Suddenly Frank's stomach growled, and Keith laughed.

"Oh, sorry," he said. "Help yourselves."

The brothers sat down quickly and began to eat.

"Where is P.J., anyway?" Joe asked as he munched on a muffin.

"He just went outside to make sure the camper is ready for today's trip."

While Frank and Joe ate, they filled Keith in about the intruder in their van and the chase through the woods the night before.

Keith looked from Frank to Joe. "Does this mean you're going to handle my case?" he asked.

"Right," Joe nodded. "We'll find out what's going on. You just concentrate on finishing your race."

"Before the race begins this morning, we want to talk to some of Gregg Angelotti's people," Frank said.

"No problem," Keith said. "They won't be hard to find. They're all staying at the other end of the trailer park."

Keith rattled off the names and descriptions of the people who were traveling with Gregg. "But Gregg won't be easy to talk to," he warned. "He likes to hide before riding—no interviews, no photos, and no exceptions."

"Oh, no! What on earth—?" P.J. suddenly shouted from outside.

Frank, Joe, and Keith rushed out and found P.J. looking into the engine of the camper.

"We don't need two young detectives," P.J. said, shaking his fist angrily at the engine. "We need a full-time guard dog around here. And a vicious one at that!"

"P.J., what's wrong?" Keith asked calmly.

They were a well-matched pair. Keith always seemed to keep cool no matter what, while P.J.'s temper was never very far from the exploding point.

"Do you see this treachery?" P.J. exclaimed, waving a thin metal wire in his hand. "This is the accelerator cable—and it's been *cut!* I can't drive this tank until it's replaced, which may take hours."

"P.J.," Frank asked quietly, "how do you know the cable was cut? Maybe it just snapped."

P.J. shook his head and took a glove out of his pocket. The palm of the glove was smooth black leather, but the back was dotted with small "breathing" holes.

"Because I found *this* where it doesn't belong—in the engine!" he said. "Just exactly where the person who cut the cable dropped it!"

4 Suspect Number One

Keith would have to start this leg of the race alone, without P.J. following in the camper. Frank and Joe didn't like that situation any better than Keith did.

"We'll just have to be doubly sharp," Joe said, trying to reassure Keith.

"That's it, lads," P.J. chimed in. "You keep your eyes peeled and take good care of him until I get there."

It was agreed that Frank and Joe would carry Keith's food, water, first-aid kit, and some minimal bicycle repair equipment in their van when the race started. They'd follow along with the caravan of trucks and campers that accompanied Keith and Gregg. P.J. would catch up with them when their camper's accelerator cable was fixed.

"How long until the race starts?" Frank asked Keith.

"About an hour. Why?"

"Because until then, Joe and I have some investigating to do. We're going to find out who owns that glove."

The glove traded pockets, from P.J.'s to Frank's. Then Frank and Joe walked past the uniform rows of motor homes and RVs, toward the south end of the park.

When they came to the group of campers belonging to Gregg Angelotti and Am-Bike, they stopped. There, everything was different. There were more people bustling around, and the equipment was more high-tech and expensive. But the main attraction, the rider himself, was nowhere in sight.

A young woman was sitting in a director's chair right outside Gregg's camper door. Her long chestnut-colored hair was pulled back in a ponytail clip. She was writing on a laptop computer, and she seemed lost in her own thoughts.

Frank and Joe knew from Keith's description that this was Suzy Burgo. She was a public relations writer hired by Am-Bike to arrange all of Gregg's TV and radio interviews. She also wrote press releases about Gregg for the newspapers and magazines.

As Frank watched Suzy's fingers skip across the computer keyboard, he decided to try a surprise technique to catch her off guard.

Standing in front of Suzy, Frank dropped the thin black leather glove down onto her computer without saying a word.

"Are you giving me a present or challenging me to a duel?" Suzy asked without looking up.

"I'm returning a glove," Frank said.

Suzy tilted her head up, pushed her round sunglasses back on her forehead, and looked at Frank and Joe.

"It's not mine," she said.

"I didn't say it was," Frank replied, sitting down uninvited in a director's chair next to her.

"It's Gregg Angelotti's, isn't it?" Joe said.

The mention of Gregg's name brought color to Suzy's cheeks, and she seemed to raise her guard a little more. "No, it's not Gregg's glove," she said sharply. Then she lowered her head and went back to her writing.

"How do you know?" Frank asked.

"Cyclists' gloves have the fingertips cut off," Suzy explained, giving the glove back to Frank. "If you had done your homework, you'd know that's a driver's glove. You're reporters trying to interview Gregg, aren't you?"

"I'm just trying to return a lost glove," Frank said.

"Okay. Then maybe it belongs to Miguel," Suzy said.

Frank and Joe knew she meant Miguel Hailey, Gregg's trainer, whom Keith had described quite graphically. Miguel's nickname in the bodybuilding business was the Compactor, because he could break a weak athlete as easily as a trash compactor could squeeze an aluminum can.

"Miguel has a sports car, and sometimes he wears driving gloves," Suzy said. "But he didn't bring the car along on this tour."

"Was Miguel here all morning?" Joe asked.

"You're asking too many questions," Suzy snapped. "If you're not reporters, who are you?"

At times like this, Joe wished he and his brother had something that looked like a private investigator license. But neither he nor Frank answered her. Instead, Frank just went on with his verbal attack.

"This glove was found in the engine of Keith Holland's camper, right where his accelerator cable was cut," Frank said. "And last night someone tried to break into Keith's camper. Know anything about that?"

"I had no idea that Bayport was such a crime-ridden city," Suzy said with a half-smile. "And are you asking all these questions as concerned citizens of Bayport?"

Joe and Frank nodded.

"Sure," Suzy said skeptically. "You know what? I think you guys have some connection with Keith Holland. So let me give you a word of advice. I may not look very big, guys, but my hands are lethal weapons." She held her hands up and turned them over a couple of times—backs, palms, backs, palms. Then she set them down, her fingers poised on the computer keys.

"All I have to do," she went on, "is write one story that Keith Holland is flipping out, accusing innocent people of trying to do him in. Newspapers all over America will eat it up. Is that what you want?"

"All *we* have to do," Frank countered, "is tell the papers that no one knows where Gregg Angelotti was last night when Keith's camper was almost burglarized. Or where he was this morning when Keith's accelerator cable was cut."

"The way we see it, Gregg is the number one suspect," Joe added. "He's got the most to gain if Keith drops out of the race."

"Gregg Angelotti has been resting in his camper since we arrived in Bayport yesterday," Suzy said in an angry but official tone of voice. "This tour is exhausting, you know, and he has to rest to let his muscles heal."

"And where were *you* last night?"

"Me?" Suzy said with surprise in her voice. "I went into New York City last night."

"So you don't really know if Gregg was in his camper the whole time or not," Frank said.

"I've already told you that isn't Gregg's glove," Suzy said. "We don't have anything more to talk about."

"She's right, Joe. Let's ask Gregg ourselves," Frank said.

"You want to talk to Gregg?" Suzy said, standing up and tucking the computer under her arm. "Then you go and wait at the finish line in Bangor, Maine. He'll be there, and that second-rate racer Keith Holland won't!"

31

Joe motioned to Frank with his head that it was time to leave. Frank looked frustrated, but he stood up and walked away from Gregg's camper for a quick conference with his brother.

"I've got a plan," Joe said. "I'll be right back." He sprinted off toward the other end of the trailer park.

About five minutes later, Joe returned tossing a football the brothers always kept among the stuff in the back of their van.

"What are you going to do with that?" Frank asked as he followed Joe into a grassy recreation area about twenty feet away from Gregg's trailer.

"Just go out for a pass," said Joe. "And whatever you do, don't catch anything I throw."

So Frank went down and out, he did button hooks, he ran all over the grassy clearing. Joe zipped bullet after bullet to him, and every one went through Frank's hands, on purpose.

After each dropped pass, Joe shouted something like, "What's the matter with you?" "Do you need a catcher's mitt?" "Do you have a hole in your hand?" "Do you need a ball with training wheels?"

The Hardy brothers were getting their exercise, but they didn't seem to be getting closer to Gregg Angelotti—until a voice suddenly called out from behind them. "Hey, you're not bad!"

Frank and Joe looked over to see Gregg Angelotti standing there in sweatpants and a sweatshirt. He was all alone.

"I was in the camper back there," he said, walking toward them. "But I can hear the thump of a football hitting someone's chest ten blocks away."

Frank smiled to himself. His brother's plan had worked. The football and the competitive situation were just the bait to draw out a shark like Gregg Angelotti.

Gregg held out his hands, and Joe flipped him the ball. Gregg squeezed it hard between his hands. It was obvious that Gregg Angelotti was the kind of guy who constantly tested the endurance of everything—a football, a bicycle, another rider, and himself.

"It feels good to get out of my camper and do something besides ride a bike," Gregg said.

Joe went out for a pass, and Gregg threw him a long bomb.

"Hey, you've got a pretty good arm on you," Joe called, lobbing the ball back toward Gregg. "I'll bet you're even strong enough to break one of these camper door handles without using a tool."

"What's that supposed to mean?" There was a hot, angry edge to Gregg's voice.

"Let me ask you something, Gregg. Did you leave your camper last night?" Frank said.

"It's a camper, not a jail," Gregg snapped. "Who are you guys, anyway?"

"We're asking around because there was a break-in in the trailer park last night," Joe explained.

"And you want to know if I did it?"

"Maybe we just want to know if you heard anything," Frank said, trying to keep the lid on Gregg's volcano.

"Gregg!" Suzy Burgo called, coming around the back of the camper. "There you are. Those two guys work for Keith Holland!"

When Gregg heard that, he grabbed Frank by the shirt and started pushing. They glowered at each other.

"I don't like jokers," Gregg said.

"I can wrinkle my own shirts," Frank said. "I don't need any help. So let go."

Frank put his hands on Gregg's wrists and started to push back.

"You guys aren't cops, that's for sure," Gregg said.

Suzy grabbed Gregg's arm and tried to back him away from Frank. Finally, Gregg let go of Frank's shirt.

"We're just two guys trying to find out why Keith Holland has been having so many 'accidents' during this race," Frank said.

"Maybe he's just unlucky," Gregg sneered, pulling away from Suzy and walking back toward his camper.

"I think with Frank and me around, Keith's luck is going to change," Joe called to him.

But, unfortunately, Joe hadn't read the morning paper before making that prediction.

Suddenly Keith Holland came marching down the path carrying a small stack of newspapers.

34

Behind him was P.J., followed by two other men. One was a muscular giant with a sharp, angular face and black hair cut short. This had to be Miguel "The Compactor" Hailey, Gregg's trainer. The other was a bearded, balding man carrying a video camera on his shoulder. He was wearing a press tag that said "Dave Luckey—SportsTalk Today." That was the name of a well-known syndicated TV sports program.

When Keith reached the spot where Frank, Joe, and Suzy were standing, he yelled, "This is the last straw, Angelotti! I've had enough of your dirty tricks and cheap shots!"

Gregg whirled around angrily.

"Listen, Keith," Suzy Burgo said quickly. "Every time you and Gregg even look at each other, it's bad publicity for the race. Now back off."

"This isn't a social call," Keith said sarcastically. "I'm just delivering the newspaper. Take a look at the front-page headline!"

With that, he threw copies of the Bayport morning paper on the ground.

Frank picked up one of the newspapers and read the headline in disbelief. In big, large, black type, it said:

FAMOUS PSYCHIC PREDICTS:

KEITH HOLLAND WILL NEVER FINISH
BIKE-AID RACE!

5 The Attack on Keith

Gregg walked over, picked up a newspaper, and read the headline. "Now, this is dynamite publicity! I'm going to read this every day right before my warm-up." He grinned. "I'll bet your stomach feels like it's wrapped in handlebar tape right now, Keith, old buddy."

Gregg and Miguel laughed, but Keith was a bomb ready to explode. Meanwhile, Dave Luckey kept his video camera rolling, taping the entire thing.

P.J. was surprisingly calm about the whole situation. "Let's get out of here, Keith," he said quietly. "You know it's all just part of the game. Ride your own race, that's all, and show them who's tough out there, *on the road.*"

But Keith wasn't ready to leave—not until he'd had an explanation for the psychic's prediction. He turned to the Hardy brothers. "Tell me

36

Molly Frankel's a crackpot, a nut, a joke," Keith begged them. "Tell me she gets her information from reading tea leaves."

"We can't tell you that," replied Frank. "We know her a little. She's always been legit."

"You're a big help," Keith said glumly.

"Listen, Keith, I've got an idea," Joe said, wrapping his arm around Keith's shoulders and pulling him aside. "I'll call Molly right now, and we'll find out what her story is so you can get on with the race. How about it?"

P.J. seconded the motion, saying, "Right, lad. You've got to get on with the race."

Keith agreed, and he, Joe, and P.J. went off to make the call before it was time for Keith to start warming up.

"If you talk to that psychic," Gregg shouted at Keith's back, "ask her if I'm going to get a movie deal from winning this race! Ha ha ha."

"I need a walk," Suzy Burgo said, and she left.

Miguel signaled to Gregg that it was time for him to start his warm-ups.

Gregg flopped down on the grass and slowly brought his legs up over his head. His toes touched the ground behind his head while he balanced his weight on his arms, which were straight out in front of him. Finally, he brought his legs back over and rested them flat on the ground.

"Good." Miguel nodded. "Again."

Gregg was all work now, so Frank decided to

pack up whatever equipment P.J. wanted them to carry in their van. He walked through the trailer park, passing row after row of trailers and campers.

Suddenly he came to an empty trailer stall, a twelve- by twenty-foot gravel area with clumps of grass sprouting up here and there among the pebbles. This particular parking area also had Suzy Burgo sitting in the middle of it. She held a bushy orange tiger cat on her lap.

Frank stopped and stared down at Suzy. Then he eased himself onto the ground next to her.

"My new friend and I are having a very enjoyable conversation," Suzy told the older Hardy brother. "Don't spoil it."

"You disappeared before I got a chance to ask what you thought about the newspaper head-line," Frank said.

"I don't think anything about it," Suzy replied, gently stroking the cat under its chin. "Am-Bike pays me to keep Gregg's name *in* the papers and to keep Keith's name *out* of the papers, if you follow me. That psychic's predic-tion was a big surprise."

"A surprise? Maybe. But you've got to be happy about it," Frank said.

"Yeah, sure," Suzy answered without enthusi-asm.

The cat twisted its head to the side so that Suzy could get a better angle to rub its neck. She petted the cat and asked Frank a question with-out looking at him. "As a loyal son of Bayport," she said, "tell me, who is this psychic, Molly What's-her-face?"

"Molly Frankel. She's a psychic and a local celebrity," Frank explained. "She gets visions. A lot of people laughed her off at first. But after she found some lost kids, missing money, and even solved a few murders, people and the police stopped laughing and started listening to her."

"Then her prediction could come true," Suzy said. "That's too bad for your friend Keith Holland, isn't it?"

"Even psychics can get their wires crossed," Frank said.

Suzy shrugged. She stood up and walked away, and the cat followed her.

Thirty minutes later, the bikers and their support teams began to gather at the trailer park entrance, the starting line for the day's race. Frank had their van packed by the time Joe came back with the news.

"Molly Frankel didn't answer her phone," Joe said, leaning against the van. "And her answering machine said, 'You don't have to leave a message because I already predicted you would call.'"

"I'll bet Keith didn't see the humor in it," Frank said.

Joe just rolled his eyes.

Just then, Frank noticed Miguel standing off by himself. He quickly crossed the road to talk to him.

"I wanted to give you back your glove," Frank said, handing Miguel the incriminating black leather driving glove.

"Thanks," Miguel said. He glanced at it and stuffed it in the back pocket of his sweatpants.

"You'll never guess where you lost it," Frank said. "In the engine of Keith Holland's camper."

For a big man, Miguel moved his arms pretty fast. He practically ripped his pants yanking the glove out of his pocket, then he threw it at Frank's feet. "It's not mine," Miguel said quickly. "I made a mistake. It's not mine."

"Miguel—" Frank started to say. He wanted Miguel to try on the glove.

"This conversation is over," the trainer said, walking away.

Frank picked up the glove and once again put it back in his pocket.

"We're having a tough time finding someone to claim that glove," Frank said as he walked back to Joe.

Instead of answering, Joe suddenly poked his brother in the side and pointed toward the starting line. Gregg was talking to Keith, and even from a distance it was clear he was saying something that made Keith angry.

Frank and Joe hurried over to see what was happening. But by the time they got there, Gregg had walked away toward his bike.

"What's going on?" Joe asked P.J.

"That guy has some nerve," P.J. said hotly.

40

He pointed an accusing finger at Gregg. "It's bad enough that Keith was injured the other night. But who needs that conceited creep coming over here and rubbing our noses in it?"

By now, Keith was back to calm and cool. He climbed onto the Silver Star and clamped his shoes into the pedals. "You have to get used to Gregg," Keith said. "Sometimes he forgets that races are won with bikes and not with his mouth."

"Well, you teach him differently," P.J. said. Then, he added as an afterthought, "And be careful. Remember everything I ever taught you. Be sure to drink lots of water—water is everything on the road. And don't take chances with your leg. You've got to baby that injury, you know."

Keith nodded his head to everything his trainer said.

At exactly seven A.M., the racers kicked off, riding toward the rising sun along a low-traffic highway. Gregg, pedaling at a steady 90 rpm, tried to break away and quickly open a big gap. Keith and the Silver Star accepted the challenge and matched his pace.

The support teams stayed well behind. They formed a small caravan of campers and vans in the right lane of the four-lane highway. The first truck in the line was the video van, which someone drove while Dave Luckey sat buckled into a special seat welded to the roof of the truck.

41

Last in line was the dark blue police van belonging to Frank and Joe Hardy.

The racers seemed to take turns sprinting ahead and catching up with each other. But actually, this was their way of keeping a constant pace.

"This is like the old days, when we were on teams together," Gregg called out as he came even with Keith. "You'd set the pace, lead the pack, and then at the end, I'd sprint across the finish line!"

"These aren't the old days!" Keith shouted, pulling ahead.

Gregg moved forward to the tip of his seat and really leaned into a vigorous sprint. "Hey! Here come some hills. You'd better baby your bad leg," Gregg taunted as he passed his opponent one more time.

Hills were a cyclist's worst enemy. Eighty or ninety rpm were hard enough to maintain on level roadway, hour after hour, mile after mile. Keeping a constant rhythm over hills was even harder. Usually, going uphill required shifting to lower climbing gears. It also took more energy and a stronger push.

But it was on hills that the unconventional gears of the Silver Star really met the challenge of the race. The bike was designed to take hills without having to shift to the lowest gear.

"I'll show you whose leg needs babying," Keith shouted. Without shifting down, he started to sprint forward. He knew that this was

42

a perfect opportunity to show everyone how well the Silver Star could perform.

Keith caught up with Gregg on the first hill, then he passed him and kept climbing. His legs seemed to move effortlessly. Then, to everyone's amazement, Keith just disappeared over the crest of the hill. Gregg and all the trucks in the caravan were left behind.

"Way to go, Keith!"

Frank and Joe were cheering from inside their van. But suddenly their cheers were interrupted by the unmistakable sound of a gunshot. It had come from just over the next hill!

Instinct took over. Joe floored the gas pedal, and the van swerved into the left lane, passing all the trucks and campers in the caravan to get over the hill.

There they found Keith Holland lying facedown in the middle of the road, a small puddle of blood near his face.

6 A New Angle

Joe and Frank held their breath as they knelt down by Keith.

Very carefully, Joe turned Keith onto his back. They both sighed with relief. Keith hadn't been shot. The blood was from a small cut on his forehead.

One by one, the other members of the Bike-Aid entourage began arriving.

Gregg, who had been right behind Keith, was first. "What happened?" he asked, sounding genuinely concerned.

"We don't know," Frank answered. "He's breathing, but he seems to be unconscious."

"But where's his bike?" Gregg asked.

Frank looked around and suddenly felt as though a brick had hit his stomach. Gregg was right—the Silver Star was gone!

Soon Suzy, Miguel, and Dave Luckey arrived, along with the two men who had been driving their trucks. They all stood around Keith, wondering what to do. Just as Suzy was about to go call an ambulance, Keith came to with a groan. He opened his eyes and focused them on Frank and Joe.

"What happened?" Joe asked.

Keith shook his head hard, trying to clear his thoughts. "It all happened so fast. I heard a gunshot and lost control of my bike," he said, sitting up slowly. "I knew *I* wasn't hit, so I guess they shot my tires. I flipped over the handlebars and hit the road—the hard way."

"Why do you say 'they'?" Frank asked.

"There were two of them. I was okay when I hit the ground, but then two guys wearing ski masks came from the trees by the side of the road. They clamped a cloth to my face, and after that I remember zip."

"They probably gave you a dose of chloroform," Frank told him.

"I don't get it," Keith said. "Why would anybody—"

All of a sudden, Keith looked around and realized his bike was missing.

"Oh, no, no, no . . ." Keith moaned. "Michael Saperstein is going to kill me." Then he turned his eyes toward Gregg. "Angelotti, if you had anything to do with this—"

"Give me a break, Keith."

"Okay, but I'll tell you something. Silver Star or no Silver Star, I'm going to finish the race if I have to ride a unicycle!"

"Tough guy," Gregg said. "Go get your head patched up, will you? The race can wait."

"And I want my bike back," Keith said to Frank and Joe. "Find the Silver Star for me."

"Will do," Joe said, slowly raising his right fist as a sign of determination.

Keith stood up and went to Gregg's camper to put some ice on his head.

Twenty minutes later, P.J. arrived in the patched-up camper. A few minutes after that, the police arrived in the tall, thin form of Officer Con Riley. He stepped into Keith's camper and said, "I should have listened to you a little harder, huh, kid? Trouble has been shadowing you for days. Let's sit down, and you can tell me what you know."

Keith, P.J., and the policeman were enough company for the size of the camper, so Frank and Joe waited outside.

Finally, Con Riley sent Keith out and called the Hardy boys in. Frank and Joe filled him in on what had been happening and told him about the evidence they had collected—what there was of it.

"Footprints running away from the camper, a broken accelerator cable, and a driving glove," Con Riley said. "Let me say this about your evidence, boys—it's a little on the thin side, don't you think?"

46

"We know it's thin, Con," Frank said. "But we were just getting started."

"Don't forget someone broke into our van last night, too," Joe added.

The police officer shook his head. "But you can't connect that with what's been happening to Keith Holland," he said. "However, that bike theft needs looking into. I'm going to check out the area where the Silver Star was stolen, but Keith hasn't given me much to go on. Sounds like a very professional job, though."

He walked to the door of Keith's camper, then stopped. "You know, I always wanted to buy one of these big babies," Con Riley said, rubbing his hand on the camper's simulated wood wallboards. "I'd fill it up with videotapes of all my favorite old movies, and you wouldn't see me for months."

"I'll bet you do it someday," Joe said.

The policeman walked out the door. "Good luck," he said over his shoulder.

"Thanks, Con," said Frank. "And thanks for the idea."

Joe's head snapped in the direction of his brother. "Idea?" Joe said. "What idea?"

"Videotapes," Frank said, pushing his brother out the door. "I'll bet Dave Luckey has some pretty interesting footage of what happened to Keith, don't you?"

A minute later, Frank and Joe were knocking on the door of Dave Luckey's mobile video van. Finally, Dave came out.

"It's awful, isn't it?" Dave said sadly.

"Yes, it is," Frank said.

"It's really awful," Dave repeated. "I keep asking myself how I could let it happen."

"Hey, what happened to Keith isn't your fault, Dave," Joe said.

Dave's eyebrows rose. "I'm not talking about that!" he said. "I'm talking about the fact that I didn't get any of it on tape! I was half a mile away when it happened. It would have been perfect for my show."

"Is that all you care about?" Joe said hotly. "Your show?"

"Cool it, Joe," warned his brother. "Remember why we're here." Then he turned to Dave and asked the journalist if he'd show them whatever videotape he had shot that morning. Maybe—just maybe—there was something useful on it.

"Show you my tapes? Are you crazy?" Dave sputtered. "Nobody sees my tapes. I'm not even showing Am-Bike a rough cut."

"The police will want to see them," Frank pointed out. "Look, Officer Riley was here just now, investigating the theft of the Silver Star. He's a friend of ours, and he knows we're working for Keith Holland. So we'd really appreciate it if you'd help us out."

"Okay, okay," Dave said quickly. "You can see the tapes. But I want a deal with you guys." Dave went on to say that he would show them the tapes if Frank and Joe promised to call him—and only him—when they found the people who had stolen the Silver Star.

"You don't call the local news, you don't call the networks, you call me," Dave said.

They shook hands. Dave's hand was cold.

At first the tapes didn't seem worth the trouble. Dave sat the Hardy brothers on swivel chairs in front of a wall full of TV equipment and monitors. The first cassette he played had scenes he'd shot that morning before the race. The second showed the beginning of the race. In the third tape, the racers were on the highway and moving farther away from Dave's camera. Keith sprinted well ahead and went over the hill.

"I stopped rolling tape after I couldn't see them," Dave explained. "Tape is expensive, you know."

They played the third tape again, studying it more carefully.

"Do you see what I see?" Joe said suddenly, leaning closer to the monitor.

"Yeah—that truck. It's driving too slowly."

They played the tape again, and even Dave leaned in to see what they were looking at.

The tape showed Keith pulling up the hill. But there was another vehicle on the road, traveling in the same direction. It was a red-and-blue Easy-Haul truck, and it seemed to be following Keith in the left lane. Then it sped past Keith and disappeared quickly over the hill before Keith reached the top.

49

"I can't see the license plate," Joe said, squinting his eyes. "It's too small."

But Dave, who was always ready to show off his high-tech equipment, said he could fix that. He put the videocassette into a projection TV and hit the close-up button. This time, when they watched the truck pass by, they could read its license plate clearly.

"Well?" asked Dave after the tape was over.

"Well, what if the bike thieves were in that truck?" Frank answered. "And when they saw Keith break away—"

"—they sped ahead of him and hid the truck in the trees next to the highway," Joe said, picking up Frank's line of reasoning. "They waited to ambush Keith. And when he came over the hill, they shot his tires and rushed out of the woods to chloroform him."

"Then they threw the Silver Star into the Easy-Haul truck and took off at top speed," Frank said.

He and Joe looked at each other with a knowing gleam in their eyes. It fit.

"You guys could never make it as detectives," Dave said with a laugh. "That's the most unbelievable story I've ever heard—and I've done a lot of television."

Unbelievable or not, it was the only lead Frank and Joe had to go on. They thanked Dave for his help and rushed out of the video van, almost knocking P.J. over in his tracks. P.J. had come looking for Frank and Joe with news of his own.

"Keith has been making some alterations on his spare racing bike, and he's ready to get back on the road," P.J. said.

"Where is he? We've got to talk to him."

P.J. led Frank and Joe across the road to where Keith was testing out his bike and getting himself psyched up to ride again.

"You know, I'm not superstitious," Keith said, "but I can't stop thinking about that psychic— what's her name?"

"Molly Frankel. Why can't anyone remember her name?" Frank asked his brother.

"Right—Molly Frankel," Keith went on. "Anyway, I'm kind of freaked out by this whole scene. She says I won't finish the race, and then this happens. Do you think she knew someone was going to steal the Silver Star?"

Frank and Joe looked at each other with one of those "That never occurred to us" looks.

"We'll check her out," Frank promised. "And we also have a lead on someone—or a truck, at least—that might have been involved. So I think Joe and I had better stay here in Bayport for the next day or so, to follow up these leads."

"It makes sense to me," Keith said. "Since the Silver Star was stolen here, the thieves might still be somewhere around. But I wish one of you could come along on the tour with me anyway. You wouldn't consider splitting up, would you?"

51

"We'd rather not," Joe said.

"Okay. I'll keep in touch," Keith said, hopping onto the bike he was going to ride until the Silver Star was found.

From there, the Bike-Aid tour was on its way to New York City for two days. The riders would rest in a hotel and spend their time doing TV interviews to promote Bike-Aid.

Frank and Joe, on the other hand, were headed for the Easy-Haul rental office in Bayport. Joe checked the clock on the dashboard in their van. "We'd better make tracks," he said to Frank. "The Easy-Haul office closes in half an hour."

Joe drove as quickly as the law allowed. But all of a sudden he and Frank saw something that might save them the trip into town.

A large red-and-blue Easy-Haul truck was barreling down the road in the opposite direction. And apparently the speed limit was the farthest thing from the truck driver's mind.

7 Another Prediction

Joe whipped the van around at the next light and took off in pursuit of the speeding Easy-Haul truck.

"Guess what?" Frank said, looking through a pair of binoculars. "There's no license plate on the back of that truck."

"This could be it," Joe said excitedly. "They probably took the plates off to disguise the truck!"

"Don't lose them—let's go!"

The Easy-Haul sped on, driving wildly for mile after mile. When the truck turned right, Joe turned right. When the truck turned left, Joe turned left after it. Finally, the truck slowed down as it neared a stoplight at the outskirts of Bayport. Joe zipped in front of the truck and cut it off.

Jumping out of the van, Joe and Frank ran up to the door of the Easy-Haul and yanked it open. There, behind the wheel of the truck, sat red-haired, green-eyed Melanie Challoff, a young woman Frank and Joe Hardy had known since kindergarten. Her name and the word *flaky* often came up in conversation together.

"Melanie?" Joe said. "What are *you* doing in there?"

"Well, Joe Hardy," Melanie said indignantly, "you certainly don't expect me to drive this truck from out *there*, do you?"

"Do you know you're driving a truck with no plates?" Frank asked. "That's illegal."

"That's okay," Melanie said with a broad grin. "The radio doesn't work either."

Sometimes you needed a road map to follow Melanie's logic.

It didn't take Frank and Joe very long to realize that this was not the truck they were looking for. However, it did take a while for Melanie to tell the whole story about why she had rented the truck to take a load of wooden trunks from her mother's shop to an antique show in the neighboring town of Clarksville.

While he was listening patiently, Frank got an idea.

"Melanie, was there someone else renting a truck like this at the same time as you were?" Frank asked.

"Frank and Joe, are you asking me to help you solve a case?" Melanie asked excitedly.

"Well, yes," Frank said. "I guess we are."

"Great!" Melanie shouted. "As a matter of fact, I think there *was* someone in the rental office with me."

"Was it a man or a woman?" Joe asked.

"Gee . . . I can't remember," Melanie said.

"What did he or she look like?" Frank asked.

"Um . . . gosh, Frank, I didn't notice," Melanie said.

"Well, what did the person have on or sound like?" Joe asked impatiently.

"Nothing special," Melanie answered with a shrug.

"Okay, thanks, Melanie. You've been a big help." Frank sighed.

She started the truck with a roar and shouted, "Hey, being a detective isn't as hard as I thought! Call on me anytime!" Then she drove away, her tires screeching.

Back on the road again, Joe glanced at his older brother and said, "This case isn't exactly going like Swiss clockwork."

"More like Swiss cheese," his brother replied.

By the time Joe pulled into the parking lot of Easy-Haul Truck Rentals, it was exactly 5:07 P.M. The assistant manager had left a sign in the office plate-glass window that read, "I've gone home. Why don't you?" It was signed "Charity Fleager, Assistant Manager."

There was another sign, this one on the door. It read, "Hours of Stress—8:00 A.M. to 5:00 P.M."

The information they were looking for was locked up inside the office.

Frank and Joe walked over to the chain-link fence that surrounded the parking lot. The fence was locked, but with the binoculars they were able to check out every truck on the lot. None of them had the license plate number they were looking for. That meant the truck they were looking for was still out on the road.

"We'll have to come back tomorrow. I wonder how Keith's doing?" Joe said as they drove home for dinner.

"And I wonder if Aunt Gertrude is making fried chicken for dinner," replied Frank. Aunt Gertrude, Fenton Hardy's sister, lived with the Hardy family. "I'm starving! That five A.M. breakfast with Keith seems like it happened a million years ago."

Joe felt his stomach rumble, and he pressed down on the accelerator a little harder.

Later that evening, after a delicious fried-chicken dinner, Frank filled his father in on the details of their case, hoping for an expert opinion.

"Take this case *very* seriously," was Fenton Hardy's feeling this time. "It isn't just a stolen bike—not when the thieves used chloroform on Keith. There's something bigger and uglier going on. I can feel it in my old detective's bones."

"Oh, your bones aren't *so* old, Dad," Joe said.

"If you ask me, this case sounds much too dangerous," said Aunt Gertrude, coming out of the kitchen. She was carrying a coconut cake, which she placed on the dining-room table. Frank and Joe looked at each other and rolled their eyes.

"Don't worry about us so much," Frank said. "We'll be okay."

At seven, Joe flipped on the TV to catch the news. Keith's face popped up on the screen. He was being interviewed in New York City about Bike-Aid and the stolen Silver Star. It was the same old story, though—none of the information was new to Frank or Joe.

"Keith seems like a nice young man," Laura Hardy remarked.

When the news was over, Fenton Hardy started teasing his wife about how he was going to beat her in their weekly tennis match.

"Even with your old detective bones?" Laura Hardy teased back.

Suddenly the telephone rang, interrupting the family banter.

"It's for the boys," Fenton called from the hallway.

Frank stood up. Then he paused and looked at Joe, who was eyeing the half-eaten piece of cake on his brother's plate. "If I answer the phone, I expect to find my cake still on my plate when I get back," he said.

57

"You can expect whatever you want," Joe said, unable to control his smile. "But you might be disappointed."

Frank went to the phone. "Hello, this is Frank Hardy."

"Frank Hardy," said a strong voice at the other end, "Michael Saperstein here. I designed and built the Silver Star. And Bike-Aid is my baby, too."

"Keith told us all about you," Frank replied.

"I just got off the phone with Keith," Michael Saperstein said. "It makes me mad as blazes that I'm here in Los Angeles instead of there in New York. I'd like to be there to crack a few heads together. *Then* I'd get some action."

Action was obviously the single most important word in Michael Saperstein's vocabulary and life. He went on, talking quickly. "I just wanted to let you know, I'm behind you one hundred percent. I'll pay for everything. But I want my bike back, and I want Keith Holland riding it again as fast as you can do it."

"That's what Joe and I want, too," Frank said. "Why do you think the bike was stolen?"

Michael Saperstein seemed a little surprised by the question, but he explained at length about the frenzied competition among bike manufacturers.

"I can think of a dozen bike companies who'd want to steal it and copy its design," he said. "And in alphabetical order the list begins with

58

Am-Bike. I've got another call waiting. Keep me posted."

Frank heard a click and then a dial tone. But the moment he hung up, the phone rang again.

"Hello, this is Frank Hardy."

"Good evening, Frank," said a woman's voice. It was an older voice, rough around the edges. "This is Molly Frankel speaking. I've had a vision about you and your brother." She sounded nervous, even terrified, as she spoke. "Your lives are in danger. . . . I see a cliff. . . . I see you falling. . . ."

Then the phone went dead.

8 Cliffhanger

The next day it rained hard, and there was a howling wind. Frank and Joe heard on the radio that because of the weather the Bike-Aid tour was being delayed. Keith and Gregg would stay in New York City for an additional day of publicity and some much-needed rest.

But the Hardys were not going to take it easy. Fenton was on his way to the airport to investigate a case of his own in Los Angeles, and Frank and Joe planned to return to the Easy-Haul rental office as soon as it opened.

Frank and Joe's mother sat in a window seat, watching the rain pelt the window and the wind rattle the glass.

"Well, I guess I can forget the idea of having you guys clean the barbecue grill today," she said glumly.

Joe stared at his mother. "Mom, you've already suggested that Frank and I paint the rain gutters, organize the shed, and mow the lawn—and it's pouring outside! We'd have to rent scuba equipment to do those chores today!"

"Have I suggested that you alphabetize your closets?" asked their mother.

"Why do I get the feeling," Frank said, "that you don't want us to leave the house today, Mom?"

Laura Hardy gave her two sons a steady look and said, "I don't care if you leave the house. I just don't want you going near any cliffs."

"Mom, you're not turning into a worrywart like Aunt Gertrude, are you?" Joe asked. "That's not your style."

"Look, Mom, you can't believe every prediction Molly Frankel makes," Frank said. "She's been wrong on occasion."

"Name one time," Laura Hardy demanded.

But Frank and Joe couldn't think of one.

"Don't worry," Joe reassured her. "We're only going downtown to the Easy-Haul office. There are no cliffs downtown—unless the wind is even stronger than it sounds."

Laura Hardy laughed, but Joe could tell that he had not entirely dispelled her fears. In fact, Joe felt a little uneasy himself about Molly Frankel's eerie prediction. Her track record was too good. There was no denying that she had an unexplainable gift for seeing into the future.

61

Frank pulled on his yellow windbreaker, and Joe zipped up a blue nylon jacket. Then the two of them made a mad dash from the back door into the rain. A few minutes later, they were driving toward town with an oldies tape blaring out of the cassette deck.

Frank drove into the Easy-Haul customer parking lot at exactly 8:15 A.M. According to the sign on the office door, the shop opened up at eight in the morning. But the assistant manager, Charity Fleager, didn't arrive until 9:45. She unlocked the office door, walked in, turned off the burglar alarm, and turned on the coffee maker. After that, Frank and Joe walked in.

"I hope you guys haven't been waiting long," Charity said. "I didn't think anyone would really want to rent a truck on a day like this." She shook out her raincoat with a snap of her wrist. "Great day to mow the lawn, isn't it?"

"I can't believe you said that. Did our mother call you?" Frank asked.

"No, that's just a little joke of mine. Company policy says we should try to be cheerful," Charity said. She gave a loud, ringing laugh that filled the office. "What kind of truck do you boys want to rent?"

"We don't want to rent a truck," Joe said.

"Then you should have read the big neon sign out there more carefully." Charity laughed again.

Frank explained that they were looking for

62

some information about someone who had rented a truck. Charity listened while she poured herself a cup of fresh coffee.

"I get it," she said. "You want the name, address, and telephone number of one of my customers."

"That's exactly what we want," Joe said.

"No can do, fellas," Charity said. "It's against company policy, it's against the law, and I don't think your mother would approve, either."

"I've changed my mind," Frank said suddenly. "We want to rent a truck."

"You do?"

"We do?" asked Joe, staring at his brother. Frank nodded.

Charity leaned her elbows on the customer counter in front of Frank and Joe. "Well, boys, they aren't exactly going like hotcakes this A.M., so you can pretty much have the pick of the litter. I've got a parking lot full of trucks."

"Do you have one with the license plate seven twenty-three PDE?" Frank asked.

Charity was surprised, but she was also intrigued. "Usually people order their trucks by size, not by license plate," she said, leaning closer to them.

"It's got to be that truck. I'm a very superstitious guy," Frank said.

Joe thought to himself, And you're a very clever guy, too, older brother. That's the license plate of the truck we came here looking for.

"I hope you didn't rent my lucky truck," Frank said slyly. "I've rented it before, and it's always hauled like a charm."

"Would I do that to you?" Charity said, reaching for a loose-leaf notebook.

She looked through her receipts, trying to find a rental agreement for the truck with the license plate Frank had asked for. And as she turned the pages, she absentmindedly called off the names on the receipts.

"Melanie Challoff," she muttered. "Now there's a carton of eggs for you. . . . Barney Starglow—he was here the same time Melanie was. His beard was three feet long, and half his hair was blond and the other was blue. I'll never forget him. . . . Uh-oh . . . Derek Willoughby. Bad news, guys. I rented your lucky truck to him."

"You're certain he has my truck?" asked Frank.

"*My* truck," corrected Charity. "Yep, we made a deal—he's got my truck, and I've got his passport. He's from England, and he didn't have a U.S. driver's license. So company policy says I have to keep his passport as a security deposit."

Charity closed the notebook, but not before Frank and Joe had glimpsed a passport paper-clipped to the rental agreement.

Suddenly the phone in a small inner office began to ring. Charity excused herself and went to answer it, shutting the door of the office behind her. Frank grabbed the notebook quickly, and he and Joe looked at the picture. Derek Willoughby was a man of about forty years old. His face was lean, and his dark brown hair was cut very short. His large brown eyes looked straight at the camera and seemed to dare you to look back.

Frank flipped a few pages and looked at the customs stamps. The stamp showed the date Willoughby had arrived in the U.S.—three days before.

Joe scanned the rental agreement. "It says here that he's staying at the Forty Winks Motel," he whispered to his brother.

Frank replaced the passport and the notebook just as Charity came out of the office.

"So, how about renting another truck?" she asked them hopefully. "I've got lots of lucky ones."

"We'll come back another time," Frank said.

"You don't deal well with disappointment, do you?" Charity said. "How about taking a guess at the serial number of my coffee pot. Maybe you'd like to rent that instead? It's been a slow week, guys."

Frank and Joe shook their heads and stepped back out into the rainy morning. Seagulls, driven inland by the storm, circled in the dark, clouded sky over Bayport. As he and Frank sprinted toward their van, Joe couldn't help feeling that this case was developing some dark clouds of its own.

"If Derek Willoughby wasn't in the United

States until three days ago," Frank said as he opened the van door, "that means he wasn't even in the country when Keith started having problems."

"You're right. So I guess he's not our man." Joe sounded disappointed.

Frank, too, felt disappointed, but he wasn't ready to give up entirely on their only lead. "I'd still like to know why Willoughby cruised by Keith and Gregg on the highway yesterday just before the shot was fired," Frank said. "Let's pay him a visit."

"Good idea," replied Joe as he jumped into the driver's seat. He started the engine and aimed the van for the Forty Winks Motel. The seedy motel was situated on top of a tall, steep hill in an area known for mud and rock slides. To get to it, Joe drove through the city, past Bayport's deserted beaches, and then onto a scenic road leading up a scenic hill. In the pouring rain, however, nothing was very scenic. In fact, very little was even visible.

Just as the van turned up the steepest part of the hill, the rain hit even harder. The windshield wipers were practically useless.

"I might as well be driving underwater," Joe muttered. He hunched over the steering wheel, trying to see better.

As the van climbed higher, the shoulder of the road grew narrower and narrower. The winding guardrail at the road's edge came closer to the pavement. Near the top of the hill, the guardrail was all that separated cars from a sheer drop to the beaches below.

"Headlights behind us," Joe said, checking his outside mirrors. "I guess we're not the only daredevils driving in weather like this."

Suddenly, the van jerked violently. It took a few more jolts for Frank and Joe to realize what was really happening.

"That idiot back there keeps hitting us!" Joe shouted.

The bumpers clashed together again like cymbals, but Joe gripped the wheel and held the van on its course. Then the crashing stopped—but only for a moment.

A large black car pulled alongside them. Without warning, it swerved and sideswiped Frank and Joe's van. The van skidded to the right and headed straight for the guardrail.

"Frank! I can't control the van!" Joe shouted.

As the van raced toward the edge of the road, both boys knew that they were going to go over the cliff—just as Molly had predicted!

9 The Forty Winks Motel

The guardrail would never hold back the van—not at the speed it was traveling. Joe, Frank, and the van were going to smash through the steel rail in about another twenty feet.

There wasn't time to think about bailing out. There wasn't time to think about Molly Frankel's vision turning into a real-life nightmare. There wasn't time to think, period.

Joe held on tight and let his driving sense take over. He steered into the skid, then pumped the brakes gently. Just before the front of the van hit the guardrail, he yanked the wheel to the left and brought the van to a bouncing stop right at the edge of the cliff.

For a moment neither brother moved or spoke. When they finally said something, they both talked at the same time.

"Good job," Frank said.

"Close one," Joe said.

"Don't tell Mom."

Frank unrolled his window and stuck his head out. Even the pouring rain felt good.

Why had that car tried to push them off the road? Was the driver trying to keep them from finding Derek Willoughby and the rented Easy-Haul truck? Or from finding the stolen Silver Star? Or was there a darker mystery still to be discovered?

Thanks to Joe's stunt driving, the Hardys had another chance to find out. But their van was stuck in the mud. That didn't matter much compared to just being alive, but it cost them a couple of hours of jamming cardboard and rocks under the back wheels and spinning rubber to free the van.

When they finally reached the top of the hill and the Forty Winks Motel, they looked more like a couple of special effects from a monster movie than two detectives.

The Forty Winks Motel had originally been a very attractive long ranch-style building overlooking the ocean. But the mud slides and the treacherous winding road up the hill had discouraged most customers from ever coming back. Now the motel was run-down, poorly furnished, and almost always empty. It was the perfect place for a bike thief to hide out, high atop a hill nobody ever wanted to go up, with a view of the ocean and all of Bayport.

Frank and Joe, soaked to the skin, walked into

the sparsely furnished registration office. They left a trail of water on the red plaid rug, and when they stopped, they left puddles.

The man behind the registration desk was Bill Carter, the owner of the Forty Winks. He was a short, bald man who was short on everything else, too—friendliness, patience, charm, and helpfulness.

Mr. Carter was taking care of a man and his wife who were checking out. "Did you enjoy your stay with us?" Mr. Carter asked without much interest.

"Well, to be perfectly honest," the man said, "the bed was lumpy and the shower dripped all night."

"Well, at these prices, what did you expect— the Ritz?" Mr. Carter sneered.

The couple grabbed their suitcases and hurried out the door.

"Everyone's a critic," muttered Mr. Carter as he watched them go.

Frank and Joe approached the desk.

"What room is Derek Willoughby staying in?" Frank asked.

"I don't know." Mr. Carter shrugged. Then he turned away as if that was the end of their conversation.

"I've got an idea," Joe said. There was an edge in his voice. "Why don't you look it up and tell us?"

Mr. Carter flipped through his registration book halfheartedly. "Is Mr. Willoughby expecting you?" he asked, running his finger down a list.

Joe was a little uneasy about answering that question. "Uh, sure," he said.

"I'd be very surprised," Mr. Carter said with a nasty grin. "Because there is no Derek Willoughby staying at this motel."

Frank and Joe looked at each other for a minute in stunned silence.

"You mean you don't have anyone staying here driving a rented Easy-Haul truck?" Frank asked, making sure he had heard right.

"I didn't say that," Mr. Carter said.

The brothers breathed sighs of relief. Now they were getting somewhere. In fact, when Frank and Joe described the man they were looking for—thin, fortyish, short, dark brown hair, British accent, driving a rented truck—Mr. Carter said he knew the man. But his name wasn't Willoughby. With a quick check of the man's room registration form, Mr. Carter even confirmed that the license on the truck was, just as Frank said, 723 PDE.

"That's the guy we're supposed to meet," Joe said. "What room is he in?"

"He's not staying here," Mr. Carter said.

They had come full circle. Or maybe to a dead end. "The man you describe checked out half an hour ago," Mr. Carter explained.

Of course, Mr. Carter wouldn't tell them what room Derek Willoughby, who had registered as Robert Quilt, had been staying in. But that wasn't going to stop Frank and Joe from finding out.

They left the office and wandered toward the motel units, noticing that the housekeeper had left all the doors wide open to air out the rooms.

A chambermaid came out of room 1. Frank and Joe rushed up to her.

"There's a big mess in the lobby," Frank told her. "Mr. Carter wants it cleaned up fast."

The mention of Mr. Carter got quick response from the chambermaid. She ran off without a word.

Frank and Joe quickly started their search. The first two rooms yielded no information. But in the third room they got lucky. Joe found an Easy-Haul map of Bayport in the wicker garbage pail. This had to be Willoughby's room! They searched faster, keeping one eye on the entrance so that no one would surprise them.

They checked the drawers, the closets, the desk, and under the bed, but there was nothing else. "We'd better get out of here," Joe said. His internal alarm clock was going off.

As they were leaving, Frank noticed the notepad by the telephone. The top page had a slight indentation, as if the page above it had been written on and then torn off. That meant there was an easy way to read what Derek Willoughby had written.

"Hurry," Joe said in a low voice. "The chambermaid is probably on her way back."

Frank rubbed the paper softly with the side of a pencil. Slowly, numbers began to appear in the graphite smudges. It was a phone number— 663-9723.

Suddenly, the phone on the desk rang loudly, startling Frank. He grabbed the top sheet of the notepad, and they ran out of the room.

Several minutes later, Frank and Joe sat in their van with the engine and the windshield wipers on. It had been a busy day. Willoughby had disappeared almost as if he knew Frank and Joe were coming. And the black car that had tried to run them off the road also seemed to know they were on a case—but how?

The case would have to wait, however. That night, Callie Shaw, Frank's girlfriend, was celebrating her birthday with a large party at Bayport's new Mexican restaurant, El Caballo Blanco. In a few hours, they had to pick up Callie, Chet Morton, and Chet's sister, Iola, who was Joe's girlfriend.

As Frank steered the van for home, Joe unbuckled his seatbelt and climbed into the back of the van. It wasn't the safest thing to do, but he was chilled in his wet clothes and thought there might be a dry jacket in the back.

"What are you wearing to Callie's party tonight?" Joe asked.

"A white polo shirt and that yellow cotton sweater I just bought," Frank said.

"Oh," Joe said.

It was just one word, but Frank knew immediately that it stood for more than that. "What's wrong with the yellow sweater?"

"I hate to say this, Frank," Joe said. "But it doesn't look so great on you."

"Okay, I won't wear it," Frank said. "Thanks for telling me."

"No problem. Any time," said Joe. "And since you're not going to be wearing it, could I borrow it tonight?"

Frank drove over a pothole, and the bouncing van sent Joe flying. One second he was standing in the back of the van, and the next he was sitting down holding his head.

"Are you okay?" Frank shouted.

Joe was silent for a moment.

"Are you okay?" Frank called again.

"Yeah—only I don't believe what I just found."

Joe climbed back into the passenger seat with his hand closed around something small.

"Frank, do you remember how you always used to say you hoped I'd get some sense knocked into me someday? Well, it just happened. Now I'm so smart I know exactly why we haven't been able to get anywhere with this case." Joe opened his hand. In it was a small radio transmitter. "It was stuck in the back corner on the ceiling of the van."

Frank looked at the miniature transmitter and whistled in disbelief. "So that's it—someone's been listening to every word we've said. We've been bugged!"

10 Callie's Party

"I'll bet I know when that bug crawled in here," Joe said.

"Yeah, it crawled in on that rat we found hiding in our van the first night we talked to Keith." Frank was thinking along the same lines as his brother.

Joe impulsively threw the transmitter out the window. "How do you think he latched on to us so quickly?"

"I don't know—unless it was the same person who tried to break into Keith's camper. Let's say the guy had been hanging around in the woods or something, watching the camper. Then, when we arrived, he realized we were there to help Keith and decided to bug our van."

"Well, at least now we have our first real clues. Let me see that phone number," Joe said. "I'll call it as soon as we get home."

"Why wait?" Frank said, pulling into a gas station.

Frank handed over the phone number, and Joe called it from the pay phone. He got a recording which said that the exchange was not a working one in the area.

"Another dead end," Joe reported in frustration. He and Frank agreed they would have to put the case on hold, at least until after Callie's birthday party.

Back home, Frank showered while Joe went through his closet, picking out a shirt to wear with his brother's yellow sweater. Then Joe showered and they both dressed and left for the party.

Outside, the rain had stopped and the humidity dropped off, making the night a warm and pleasant one. It was a great night for Mexican food followed by birthday cake.

"It's a beautiful night," Iola Morton said as the five of them drove toward the restaurant. Iola was wearing a pink sweater that complemented her dark hair.

She and Joe were sitting in the backseat of Laura Hardy's car, a station wagon that was much more comfortable for double dates than the old police van. Frank drove with Callie beside him—close beside him because Chet Morton was squashing her. He had insisted on sitting in the front seat next to the window. Chet had also come dressed for a Mexican costume party, complete with a large sombrero.

"You people just don't know how to fiesta," he scolded. No one could get into a party like Chet Morton.

At the restaurant, Callie took Frank's arm as they walked in. When they opened the door, voices shouted, "Happy Birthday!" and others yelled "Feliz Años!" Chet Morton asked, "When do we eat?"

Frank, Callie, Joe, Iola, and Chet led the parade of their friends toward the back room, which had been set aside for Callie's party.

But as they walked through the dark, candle-lit, crowded restaurant, a heavyset woman wrapped in a green cape passed too close to one of the tables on her way out and bumped into Joe. It was Molly Frankel, the psychic who had predicted their doom only twenty-four hours before.

"Frank and Joe Hardy!" Molly exclaimed when she recognized them. "I'm so glad you are alive! I've had such strong feelings about you!" Molly's voice was always a little gravelly, and listening to her made you want to clear your throat. "I am very glad to see that you are both safe and sound."

Joe spoke first.

"How did you know what would happen to us today?" he asked.

"I had a vision. That's all. Why are you angry with me, Joe?"

"Why am I angry? I'll tell you why—a car ran

us off the road, and we almost went flying off a cliff without parachutes."

Frank could feel Callie's hand tighten on his arm. Joe had just blurted out a story they hadn't been planning to tell Callie and Iola.

"Have you had any other dreams about us?" Joe asked. There was more curiosity in his voice than sarcasm.

"I don't have dreams," Molly stated. "I have visions of the future. And I did warn you."

Molly's face turned serious. She seemed to hesitate and then realized she couldn't hold back. "I believe a man in a dark uniform means to harm you," she said. "You must be careful— very careful."

It was a line right out of a bad movie, and if it had come from anyone else Frank and Joe might have laughed. But Molly had been right too many times.

Callie tried to pull Frank away. "What's she talking about?" she asked. "I thought you were just trying to find a bicycle."

Frank and Joe had thought it was that simple too, but not after everything that had happened on their trip to the Forty Winks Motel.

Frank could see that Molly's words were upsetting their friends. And why shouldn't they? Her words were worrying him too. So he changed the subject fast. "What about Keith Holland?" he asked Molly. "Why did you predict that Keith wouldn't finish the race?"

Suddenly Molly's expression changed. It was as if she had suddenly closed a door and locked it to keep out something that scared her.

"Goodbye, boys. Be careful," Molly said. Then she rushed out of the restaurant.

Frank and Joe wanted to follow Molly and finish the conversation about Keith.

But Callie looked at Frank and Joe with her hands on her hips. "I know you want to go after her," she said. "But if you leave and miss my birthday party the way you did last year, Frank Hardy, I'll decorate your shirt with a piece of birthday cake!"

Everyone laughed, and Frank promised Callie he would put the case of the Silver Star out of his mind for the next few hours.

After that, the party warmed up with hot and spicy nachos, and Callie opened presents and read birthday cards as Iola handed them to her. Finally, Callie came to a thin box about as long as a yardstick. It was a present from Iola—a marching-band drum major's baton. Callie's brown eyes shone with pleasure at the gift.

"Hey, Callie," someone shouted. "Don't you need a license to own one of those?"

The crowd roared with laughter, and so did Callie. Everyone was remembering that she had tried out as a baton twirler for the high school band when she was a freshman. She had been very nervous during the tryouts. And when it came time to throw the baton up and catch it, she had thrown it a little off course and broken a window in the gym.

"I thought you'd want a new one for when you start college," Iola said, giving her friend a hug.

Callie stood up, tossed her long blond hair over her shoulders, and threatened to put on a twirling show.

"No way!" people shouted. And two guys called out "Here's the best way to watch Callie twirl a baton," as they ducked underneath the table.

"Frank Hardy!" a voice called. But it wasn't easy to hear over the noise of the group. "Frank Hardy!" the voice called again.

This time Frank heard his name. "Right here," he said. But when he looked up, he almost choked on a tortilla chip.

The voice belonged to a young man wearing a dark uniform with gold buttons and red trim! "Come with me, please," the young man said.

This was fast service on Molly Frankel's prediction. "I believe a man in a dark uniform means to harm you," she had said.

"Who are you?" Frank started to say. But the man had already turned and was walking through the restaurant.

Frank got up quickly and followed him into the main dining room.

If there's going to be trouble, Frank thought to himself, I'm going to make the first move. He grabbed the man, spun him on his heels, and said harshly into his face, "What do you want with me?"

The young man looked startled and sputtered, "You have a telephone call."

Frank's eyes darted around the restaurant, and he flushed red. There were lots of other young men wearing the same uniform. They were all busboys clearing the tables.

The busboy squirmed in Frank's grip. "Hey, I'll tell the caller you're not here if that's what you want—no problem," he said.

Frank let the busboy go. "Sorry," Frank said. "It must have been the chilis rellenos."

"Yeah, right," the busboy said, pointing to the telephone and moving quickly away.

"This is Frank Hardy," Frank said into the receiver.

"Hello, Frank?" said the familiar voice of Frank's aunt Gertrude.

"Hi, Aunt Gertrude. What's up?"

"Keith Holland just called a few minutes ago," she said urgently. "The trouble has started again—only this time it's worse!"

11 Big Trouble in the Big Apple

"What happened?" Frank asked, remembering his promise to Callie.

"Keith wouldn't tell me," Aunt Gertrude replied. "But he was terribly upset. He kept saying that they were out to get him. If I'm any judge of people, I'd say Keith is about ready to crack up."

"Okay. What does he want us to do?" Frank asked.

"Go to New York right away. I'll give you the address."

Suddenly the crowd at El Caballo Blanco started cheering in the background. Frank could barely hear his aunt over the phone.

"Okay, Aunt Gertrude," Frank shouted. "I got the address. Tell Mom to use our van if she needs it because I don't know when we'll be back with her car."

"Be careful!" Aunt Gertrude cried just before Frank hung up.

Frank and Joe didn't say much as they drove into New York City. Instead, the events of the day went on instant replay in their heads. And neither of them wanted to think about Molly Frankel's new prediction.

About two hours later, they reached the West Side Highway in Manhattan and then got off near the Twelfth Avenue piers. From there, it was only a few blocks to Thirtieth Street, where Keith had said to meet him.

But when Frank and Joe drove into the dark, empty parking lot at Thirtieth Street, there was no Keith, no camper, no other cars in the lot, and no signs of life.

"Let's get out of here," Joe said. "This place gives me the creeps."

"Calm down," Frank said. "Keith's probably just late."

A metal trash can fell over somewhere in the darkness and rolled and clanked until it hit the chain-link fence surrounding the parking lot.

"Do you think Keith got lost?" Joe asked. "We could call him, but we don't know what hotel he's staying in."

Click. The sound was unmistakable. It could be only one thing—a switchblade knife springing open. Before Frank could start the engine, the whole car shook as someone leaped onto the hood.

Joe reached for the flashlight under the passenger seat and shone its strong beam into the laughing face of the man on the car hood. He was tall and young, and his brown hair was stringy. He wore a grimy T-shirt, but the knife blade he held was clean and shiny in the flashlight beam.

Sitting in a crouched position on the hood of the car, the young man shouted, "I want this car!"

"We didn't bring the title," Frank shouted back.

Suddenly a group of seven young men approached the car. One of the men stuck his head through the open window on the driver's side.

"Don't move, man, or I'll cut you."

This second voice was so close to Frank's ear that he could feel the man's breath. Frank froze, and the gang's leader jumped off the hood of the car. Quickly, Joe leaned down and flicked a toggle switch under the dashboard. Frank sighed with relief. Now all he and Joe had to do was wait. Finally, the stringy-haired man leaned his hand against the hood of the car again. And that was all it took to instantly activate the motion-sensitive car burglar alarm.

A siren under the hood screamed angrily, the headlights flashed, and the horn started blaring. It was like having a New Year's party built into your engine.

The noise and the lights froze the gang just long enough for Frank to start the engine and roar out of the parking lot, tires squealing and thick clouds of burned rubber floating behind them.

"Close one," Joe said.

They drove in search of a phone booth on a well-lighted and busy street far away from the deserted pier parking lots.

"Call Aunt Gertrude. Maybe she got the address wrong," Joe urged.

"Aunt Gertrude doesn't *forget things*," Frank reminded his brother.

"Then maybe *you* made a mistake," Joe said.

Frank laughed and gave his brother a doubting glance out of the corner of his eye. But when he got back from the phone booth, he said, "You were right. The restaurant was so noisy I got the address wrong."

The correct address was the corner of Twelfth Avenue and Thirteenth Street, not Thirtieth Street. There they found a parking lot full of campers, trailers, and vans that were too big to be kept in Manhattan's underground hotel garages.

The lot was well lit, and Keith's camper was easy to spot. But when they walked inside, Frank and Joe felt as though they were walking into an upside-down room. Furniture had been overturned and slashed, drawers emptied, closets tossed; even the food in the cupboards had been dumped out of boxes.

Keith was standing in the middle of the mess, holding the broken pieces of one of his racing trophies. He looked at Frank and Joe, hoping to find an answer on their faces. All he saw was a question.

"What happened?" Joe asked.

"I came down to the camper to get a book I wanted to read tonight," Keith said. "When I got here, the door was open and the place was a wreck."

It was more than just vandalism, Frank and Joe were sure of that. Vandals got their thrills from making a mess and leaving other people to clean it. But this was too thorough. Every inch of the trailer had been gone over carefully. Whoever did this must have been looking for something.

"Is there anything missing?" Joe asked.

Keith answered the question with one of his own. "Is there anything left?" he said.

"I always travel with everything that's important to me in the world. Books, letters, records, training journals, my trophies. Maybe it comes from being an orphan. They stole my bike, and now they've trashed my life. And I don't know why.

"I don't understand it. Is there someone who just doesn't like Bike-Aid?" Keith wondered. "Someone who doesn't want money to be raised to feed and clothe homeless people? Who would do this?" Aunt Gertrude had been right—Keith sounded like he was about to crack.

The Hardy brothers let Keith talk, because they knew that was what he needed.

"The one good thing about being an orphan,"

Keith said quietly, "is that you don't have to worry about someone stealing your book of family photos."

They let him talk a little more. Then it was time to act, before the trail cooled.

"Is there anything *specific* missing?" Joe asked.

"You're going to laugh," Keith said, prodding the mess on the floor with his foot. "Medals and trophies, my stereo equipment, TV, spare bike wheels—they're all worth something. But they didn't take those things. You know what they took? A newspaper article a friend of mine sent me. I had it taped to my closet door."

"Tell us about it," Joe prompted Keith.

"My friend David lives a couple of blocks away from me in Boulder, Colorado," Keith said. "Every week he sends me an empty envelope with a funny note on the outside that says, 'Here's what you missed in Boulder this week.' David's from Chicago, and he's not too wild about mountains and clean air."

"So?"

"So this week I got his envelope with the same message on the outside. But I was really surprised because there was something inside. It was a for-real newspaper clipping about my next-door neighbor, Marianna Bornquist."

Marianna Bornquist—it wasn't exactly a household name.

"She's a real quiet neighbor," Keith went on. "But the clipping said that a few weeks ago, the day before I started my race, a couple of black cars pulled onto her front yard, and some heavy-duty government guys took her away. It said she was under investigation for military espionage."

Military espionage? That's spying, Frank thought to himself. What did that have to do with the missing Silver Star?

"But who would want that article?" Keith asked, interrupting Frank's thoughts. "I can't believe Marianna has a fan club."

"She does now," Frank said. "And I'm the president."

Keith looked puzzled.

"At least now we have a name—someone to investigate," Joe explained.

"First thing in the morning," Frank told Keith, "we're going to find out more about Ms. Bornquist, the spy next door!"

12 Missing Cyclist

Frank and Joe drove Keith back to his room at the Plaza Hotel. Then they checked themselves into a more moderately priced hotel farther downtown.

At the crack of dawn the next day, they woke up, with the events of the previous night ringing like an alarm clock in their heads. They dressed quickly and then popped into a coffee shop to grab some orange juice and Danish for breakfast.

"Dad said it, and we've both felt it," Joe began. "There's more to this case than just a stolen bicycle."

"I agree," Frank answered between bites, "but I can't figure this latest break-in at Keith's camper. I mean, why break in to steal a newspaper clipping?"

"They didn't break in for that," Joe replied. "Keith said the clipping was in full view on his closet door. If that's all they wanted, then they didn't have to rummage through all his drawers and stuff. Right?"

"Right. So they were looking for something else, something they didn't find. But why did they take the clipping at all?"

"I don't know," Joe said, finishing his juice. "Let's find out more about Marianna Bornquist, and maybe that'll give us a clue."

So, after breakfast, the two brothers walked up Fifth Avenue to the main branch of the New York Public Library. There they read through back issues of the *New York Times* until they found what they were looking for.

It was a small story, printed a week before, about Marianna Bornquist. The *Times* had picked it up from an Associated Press writer in Boulder.

According to the article, Dr. Marianna Bornquist, a scientist and weapons designer for the government, was suspected of trying to sell secret documents on microfilm to foreign agents. What exactly was on the microfilm and whom she meant to sell it to were not spelled out in the news story. But the article did say that Marianna Bornquist had been suspended from her job and was unavailable for comment during the investigation.

"It's a great spy story," said Joe. "But we can't really connect it to Keith's troubles or to the stolen bicycle."

"Except for the fact that Marianna Bornquist

is Keith's next-door neighbor," Frank reminded Joe.

"So what?" Joe said. He looked at Frank and shrugged.

From the library, they went to the Plaza Hotel, where Frank called up to Keith's room from a lobby telephone. P.J. answered. When he heard who it was, he barked, "Get up here right away."

Seconds later, the elevator door opened onto the sixth floor, but Frank and Joe almost couldn't step out. Beyond the door was a wall of people. The narrow hallway was packed with news reporters, camera crews, and equipment.

"Give us some room." "Step back!" "No room." Voices called from everywhere.

Frank and Joe squeezed their way from the elevator into the crowd of reporters.

"You guys better come back later," a woman with a minicam on her shoulder warned the Hardys.

Another man holding a microphone and an audiocassette recorder said, "Yeah, if you don't have press passes, the cops are going to send your shoes walking."

Frank and Joe looked at each other. The police? What were the police doing here?

The door to Keith's room opened, and two men—police detectives—stepped out of the room and into the blinding spotlights and flashing strobes.

Questions came at them like machine-gun

fire. "What's the story, Lieutenant?" "What's going on?" "What about the race?" the reporters all asked at once.

Frank and Joe pushed harder toward the door to Keith's room. They still didn't know what this was all about, but they were beginning to understand P.J.'s tone of voice.

The New York City detectives dodged the questions, but they made a brief statement. "At this time," one of them said, "all we can say is that a note was found that explains the situation to our satisfaction, and we do not believe that foul play was involved."

The words, delivered so calmly, so reasonably, sent a panic through Frank and Joe. They wanted to get into Keith's room—fast.

"Hey—where are you two going?" a blue-uniformed officer asked, blocking the door.

"Joe and Frank Hardy. We just called from the lobby. We're expected," Joe said.

"Yes, I was given your names," the officer said. He let them go by.

Keith's hotel suite had a brightly lit living room, and all of the people Frank and Joe had come to know over the last forty-eight hours were sitting in it. P.J. O'Malley, Gregg Angelotti, Suzy Burgo, Miguel Hailey, Dave Luckey, and a few other Bike-Aid staff people were there. But something was wrong. No one was talking. And Dave wasn't rolling tape. His camera lay at his feet.

"Where's Keith?" Frank asked.

P.J. handed him a note, a sheet of paper torn from a lined notebook.

P.J.,
Sorry—I'm dropping out of the race. There's just too much pressure, and too many things going wrong. I'll be in touch in a few weeks, after I've had a rest. And don't worry—I'll keep training.

Keith

The Hardy brothers' stomachs dropped right into their shoes.

P.J. took the letter away from Frank, and he addressed both brothers. "Listen to me," P.J. said in a voice shaking with emotion. "I know that boy. He wouldn't do this."

The Hardys didn't believe that Keith would quit either. He was shaken up by all the trouble, but he was a champion, and champions aren't quitters. Frank and Joe immediately started looking for an explanation.

"Is it Keith's handwriting, P.J.?" Frank asked.

"It is," P.J. said. "But I'm telling you—"

Gregg Angelotti, who was standing near a window, looking out at Central Park, interrupted. "Grow up," he said. "Keith couldn't take it, that's all. It happens. There'll be other races, and maybe he'll have the guts to finish them."

P.J. glowered at the arrogant cyclist, but it was Suzy who exploded first.

"You total low-life bacterium!" she snapped at Gregg. "I've taken all I can take of you. How dare you say Keith didn't have the guts to ride this race? He rode hurt—he even rode without the Silver Star."

"Calm down, Suzy—" Gregg started to say.

"Don't tell me to calm down! If Am-Bike hadn't been paying me so much, I would have been out of here long ago. This is it, Angelotti. I quit! I'm not writing any more lies about you, you egotistical jerk!"

Everybody in the room froze, as they watched Gregg's face redden. Miguel stood up and said to Suzy, "Hey, you can't talk to Gregg like that."

Suzy shook her hair back from her face. "Miguel," she said, "maybe someday you'll learn. That's the *only* way to talk to him."

She walked toward the door, but she stopped long enough to say "Good luck" to Frank.

"I'm going to finish this race," Gregg shouted after her. "All by myself! Then everyone will know who cared about poor people and who didn't!"

Dave Luckey had been just sitting there, looking at the floor, ignoring the drama in the room and the camera at his feet. He stood up quickly and said, "I'm really sorry all this has happened." And he, too, left the room.

Gregg looked at the dwindling support team and decided he wasn't going to stick around to hear anything Frank and Joe had to say. So he told Miguel to clear a path through the reporters in the hall. The other Angelotti supporters left too.

On his way out, Gregg couldn't pass up the opportunity to make a statement to the press. "I was shocked that Keith quit the race," he said, trying to sound humble. "I'm sorry he didn't agree with me that Bike-Aid isn't a competition between him and me or between Am-Bike and the Silver Star. It's about raising money. So I'm going on to Maine alone."

Frank closed the door so they wouldn't have to listen to Gregg anymore. Then he read the note from Keith again and shook his head. It just didn't sound like Keith.

"You don't believe this?" The question was directed at P.J. as Frank held up the note.

"No way, lad," P.J. answered. "Keith wasn't a quitter."

Frank and Joe exchanged glances.

"What would you say if I told you that Keith might have been kidnapped?" Frank asked the question carefully so as not to alarm P.J.

"I'd say that ever since I saw that note, I've been waiting for the phone to ring with a ransom demand."

Right on cue, the phone rang. It had the sound of a ring no one wanted to answer, but P.J. picked up the receiver.

"Hello? Yes, Mr. Saperstein," P.J. said. "Yes,

sir. The police were here. They said they won't investigate. There is no evidence of foul play, they said." P.J.'s head drooped lower and lower the more he talked. It was as if he were a nail and Michael Saperstein were the hammer. "Yes, sir," P.J. said, looking over at Frank and Joe. "They're right here."

P.J. held out the phone toward them.

"This is Frank Hardy," Frank said.

"I just heard the worst news of my life," Michael Saperstein said. "I thought you guys were going to find my bike, not lose my cyclist."

Frank said nothing.

"I know Keith Holland better than I know my own children," Michael Saperstein went on. "He'd finish this race with both legs in casts. He was nabbed, I'll bet everything I own on that. What I want to know is, what are you going to do to find him?"

"Kidnapping is a little out of our league," Frank said. "I think you ought to contact the FBI."

"Great," Michael Saperstein said with a snort. "I'm looking for action, and the authorities have decided to sit on their hands. Now don't tell me you guys are turning your backs on me, too!"

Frank knew that what Michael Saperstein was saying was true. Because of the note Keith had left, the FBI wouldn't be willing to get involved. So far, there was no proof that Keith had been abducted.

"Frank," Michael Saperstein said, "if you and your brother are going to help me, just hang up the phone. But if you're going to walk out on me, put the phone down on the table—because I want to hear you slam the door behind you! What's it going to be, Frank?"

13 Confessions and Clues

Frank put the phone on the table for just a moment and then pressed his finger on the plunger to disconnect the phone. For a long twenty seconds, he just stood there holding the button down. Finally he spoke to P.J. and Joe.

"Kidnapping is serious business. But no one's looking for Keith, so we've got to do it."

"Thanks, lads," P.J. said, smiling. "If anyone can find him, you can."

After that, P.J. left them alone, saying, "Go ahead and search for clues or whatever you have to do." Searching for clues in Keith's suite sounded like a reasonable idea, so Frank and Joe started in the living room.

"Hey, look at this. Miguel left us an autograph," Joe said, pointing to the green velvet couch.

Miguel had sat there tensely with his palms

pressing flat on the velvet. And his hot, sweaty hands had left a perfect imprint in the soft material.

"I'm glad I stashed this in the glove compartment last night," Frank said. He dropped the driving glove—the one that P.J. had found in the camper engine—on the couch.

But it was a total mismatch. The glove was much too small for Miguel's handprint.

Frank scrunched up his mouth. "Now we know Miguel didn't cut the accelerator cable," he said.

They were about to move into the bedroom when someone knocked on the door.

Joe opened it and looked straight into the sullen face of Dave Luckey.

"Uh, I forgot my light meter," Dave said, stepping past Joe into the room. But, instead of looking for anything, he just stood there in the middle of the room.

"You didn't forget anything," Joe said.

Dave turned to look at Joe. "How do you know?"

"Because we just searched every inch of this room," Frank replied.

"You're right. Anyway, I wouldn't touch a camera that didn't have automatic aperture," Dave said. "I came back because I've got to tell someone what I've done. Keith's gone because of me."

Frank and Joe looked at each other in surprise.

"You can see it on my face, can't you? Come in on a close-up. I'm guilty," Dave said. Once he had begun, the confessions started pouring out. "I put the salt in Keith's water bottle and the glue on his handlebars. I paid a newspaper pal of mine to write some false stories about Keith. And I even paid that dippy psychic, Molly Frankel, to predict that Keith wouldn't finish the race."

"Why?" asked Frank.

"Why?" Dave said incredulously. "Because I knew if I made Keith a little nervous, I'd crank up the competitive tension, and it would make for a great TV show—that's why. But I never thought he'd take it seriously and quit."

"He didn't quit," Frank said angrily. "We think he was kidnapped."

"Kidnapped? Oh, wow," Dave said. He rubbed his face and sighed. Then his eyes lit up. "So it's not my fault after all! There's no reason for me to feel bad, is there?"

Before Frank or Joe could answer, Dave slapped the brothers on their backs. "You guys are certified life-savers, and I mean it," Dave said. "I feel great. Thanks. See ya around, fellas."

After Dave left, Joe said, "He seems like a new man."

"Are you kidding? With a guy like that, they should start from scratch," Frank said in disgust.

"Well, it's back to square one," Joe said.

"No, it's not," his brother contradicted. "In

fact, listening to Dave Luckey convinced me that we've been all wrong suspecting anyone involved with the Bike-Aid race."

Joe's face couldn't hide his surprise, and he sat down in the nearest comfortable chair. "I've got to hear this sitting down," he said.

"You heard the things he confessed to," Frank said. "Small pranks. Think about it. Would any of those people—Gregg, Suzy, Miguel—really commit kidnapping just to win a charity bike race?"

Joe shook his head. Frank was right.

"There are only two suspects in this case who aren't connected with Bike-Aid," Joe said. "Our unseen friend in the Easy-Haul truck, Derek Willoughby . . ."

"And Marianna Bornquist," Frank finished. "I don't know how she figures in this, but I'd like to find out, wouldn't you?"

Joe began to answer, but he choked back his words. A key was turning in the door.

Frank pointed to the closest closet—the living-room coat closet—and they zipped into it just before the door opened.

"This place is busier than Grand Central Station," Joe whispered to his brother in the dark.

Quick footsteps passed by the closet door, and so did a familiar odor.

"I don't hear anything now," Frank whispered. "I think he went into the bedroom."

"I smell french fries," Joe hissed.

"Give me a break. Think about food later," Frank said. He took a breath and opened the closet door a crack.

The two brothers stepped out of the closet in super-slow motion. They looked around at the empty living room. Their visitor *had* gone into the bedroom. Whatever it was the guy was looking for in there, he wasn't finding it. The sound of drawers and closets opening and slamming shut got louder as Frank and Joe moved toward the bedroom door.

The intruder's back was to them. They knew they weren't going to get a better shot than that, so they took it. Joe leaped first and grabbed the man around the middle as Frank tackled him at his feet. The three of them rolled and kicked, knocking over a table. A lamp crashed to the floor. The man couldn't move very freely because he was wearing a waiter's jacket that was much too tight. But he didn't have much fight in him anyway.

"What are you doing here?" Frank said when he and Joe had things under control.

"Haven't you ever heard of room service?" the man shouted, gasping for breath.

"Room service delivers food," Joe said.

"What do you call that over there?" the man said, trying to point with the arm Frank was twisting.

There, on a table by the bed, was a silver tray with covered dishes. Joe let go of the man and moved over to examine the food tray. He lifted

103

one of the silver lids and, with a smile at his brother, popped a french fry into his mouth.

"I suppose you were just looking around for your tip," Frank said sarcastically.

"Who are you guys?" the intruder asked. "You're not supposed to be in this room."

"Who are *you*?" Joe said, examining the room-service ticket on the silver tray. "You don't work for the hotel. This food was going to room twelve fifty-seven."

"Smart, aren't you?" the man said, shaking his head.

"We do all right," Joe said.

"Okay, I borrowed the tray," the man admitted. He reached into his pants pocket and pulled out a photo ID card. He was George Cramer, a newspaper reporter. "Can't blame a guy for trying to get a story, can you? Well, it's been real, guys."

Frank stopped the reporter with one strong hand on his chest.

"What's the idea?" George Cramer said.

Frank grabbed at a bulge in the inside pocket of the reporter's jacket and pulled out a notebook.

"It's Keith Holland's," George Cramer said. "I found it lying by his bed."

Frank and Joe knew it was Keith's because the paper in the notebook matched Keith's "farewell" note to P.J. The handwriting was the same, too.

The reporter didn't seem to mind being caught any more than he minded trying to steal the notebook. "It looks like some kind of training journal," he said casually. "It's filled with records and pulse rates and recovery times and stuff like that. I don't think it means much. Well, I'd better be on my way."

This time, Frank and Joe let George Cramer leave.

"You know," Joe said, "if I were going off somewhere to train, I'd never leave my training journal behind."

"Who said Keith went somewhere to train?" Frank asked.

"*He* did—in his note." Joe retrieved the note from the living room and read it out loud. "He says right here, 'Don't worry, I'll keep training.' It's the last thing he wrote."

"Let me see that," Frank said. "Joe, you're a genius! He must have left his training journal behind on purpose to tell us that his note was a lie! He even wrote the note on the same paper so we'd get it."

"But who made him write the note?" Joe asked.

They were back to their two prime suspects, one of whom was also the government's prime suspect in an espionage investigation.

"We can't ask Keith," Frank said. "And we can't seem to find Derek Willoughby. So why don't we ask Marianna Bornquist?"

Frank picked up the telephone by Keith's bed. After flipping through the phone book, he dialed quickly.

"Long-distance information. For what city?" asked the operator.

Frank asked for Boulder, Colorado, and the number for Dr. Marianna Bornquist. He wrote the seven digits down as she gave them to him. Joe was standing over his brother's shoulder, watching as he wrote.

"Frank! I don't believe it!" Joe said, grabbing the paper from his brother's hands. "We've had that number since yesterday."

Joe reached into his pocket and unfolded a piece of paper, the paper they had taken from Derek Willoughby's room at the Forty Winks Motel. It had the same phone number written on it—Marianna Bornquist's phone number!

14 In Search of a Spy

"Ladies and gentlemen, this is Captain Sterling speaking. We're about to make our initial approach into Boulder Airport." The captain's calm, confident voice made the passengers feel as though they were only three feet off the ground instead of thirty thousand.

Frank and Joe looked out the window of the jet. The scenery below had changed from flat yellow and green midwestern farms to the jagged peaks of the Rocky Mountains. It was almost as if the dramatic changes in landscape were mirroring the ups and downs of the case they were working on.

"You know," Frank said, "Dr. Bornquist might not be home when we get there. Anyway, she sure wasn't answering her phone. I tried it thirty-two times."

"I know. But coming out here was our only shot," Joe said. "And my guess is we're going to find out a lot in Boulder. I mean, Keith lives next door to Dr. Bornquist, so if he really *did* walk out on Bike-Aid, we just might find him there."

After the plane touched down, Frank and Joe looked for a cab in the line waiting outside the airport. About six cab drivers were standing in a group, passing around a waxed bag of doughnut holes, a local delicacy. One of the drivers noticed Frank and Joe right away and walked over to them quickly. "Howdy, gents," he said. He was a tall, thin man wearing a western hat.

"I'm Buck. Where are we going?" he asked them. He steered the brothers into his banged-up yellow cab.

"Laurel Pond," Frank said. They had gotten Keith's address from P.J. before leaving for Boulder.

"That's one of those new townhouse developments that's sprung up around here," Buck said as he drove out of the airport. "Do you have a friend living there?"

"We won't know that until after we get there," Frank said.

"Whatever you say," Buck said, flooring the gas pedal.

Frank lowered the window of the speeding cab to feel the sharp, dry mountain air and watch the friendly city of Boulder go by. Eventually, the cab turned up a twisting road, and they entered a townhouse development with rows of two-story attached houses spread out in every direction. The Oakwood section, where Marianna and Keith lived in adjacent houses, was far up the hill.

Frank and Joe had come to Boulder to talk to Marianna Bornquist, but as soon as Buck stopped the cab they went to Keith's house first. They had to know if he was there. They rang the bell several times, but there was no answer. They peeked in the windows and saw that Keith's plants were dying. The house looked as if no one had been there in a long time.

"He's not here," Joe said.

"I don't know whether to be glad or not," Frank said.

Because the two modern houses were attached, Marianna's front door was only a few feet away from Keith's. Frank and Joe repeated the routine—they rang her doorbell, peeked in the windows, and concluded that she wasn't home.

"Let's have a look around," Joe said.

They walked around to the back of the building, where balconies jutted out over the sloping ground, and boosted themselves onto the railings. From there, they were able to see into Marianna's house through the sliding glass doors.

Joe hopped onto the deck and tried the door handle. He gave the handle a shove and got a surprise—the door slid open! Frank joined his brother on the deck, and the two stepped inside the house.

"Hello! Dr. Bornquist!" Frank called.

The living room was well furnished with lamps, comfortable couches, and chairs, but the Hardys immediately noticed that something was wrong.

"Lots of bookshelves and no books," Frank said. "Closet doors open, but the closets are empty. Dishes but no food in the kitchen cupboards."

"I don't get it," Joe said. "Does she live here or not?"

"She lives here, but she's been gone for a while. Maybe she took her stuff with her, or maybe the government impounded it," Frank said. He took a step farther into the house.

"What are you doing?" Joe asked.

"I don't know," Frank said. "We've got to find something, anything, that will tell us where Keith is."

On the fireplace mantel, they found photographs in frames. Old photos showed Dr. Bornquist as a child and as a teenager posing with a large woman and a man with a bushy beard and kind eyes—probably her mother and father. In a recent photo, taken at her job, they saw that she was a tall, blond woman in her forties.

Ding dong!

The doorbell rang. Frank and Joe froze and stared at each other. Who could it be?

Ding dong!

Don't panic, they thought to themselves. Whoever it is will go away.

Knock knock . . . ding dong!

It was obvious that whoever was at the door had no intention of leaving.

Joe carefully moved a curtain aside and peered out the living-room window.

He was relieved to see that the quiet neighborhood had not been invaded by SWAT teams. There was only a single delivery truck parked in the driveway.

"It's a delivery woman, and her truck says Mannie's Electronics," Joe reported. "And she's got a small carton under her arm."

The carton was too intriguing to pass up.

"Let's take a chance," Frank said, moving toward the door to open it.

The delivery woman was wearing mirrored aviator sunglasses, blue jeans, a red T-shirt, and a baseball cap that said "Mannie's Electronics. Our low, low prices will shock you."

At first, she was surprised when the door opened, but then she asked, "Is Marianna here?"

"No," Frank said. "She's out."

His answer brought a disappointed and irritated look to the young woman's face.

"Well, do you know when she'll be back?" she asked.

"I wish I did," Frank said.

She pushed her cap back on her forehead.

"I've never seen you guys before," she said. "Are you friends of Marianna's?"

"Uh, we're from out of town," Joe said with a smile.

Frank and Joe looked around past the young woman to the street and saw that Buck had gone. The street looked deserted.

"She's in a real mess, isn't she?" the young woman said.

"It looks that way, doesn't it?" replied Frank.

The young woman started to leave, then changed her mind.

"Hey, guys, could you do me a big favor?" she asked, smiling as she turned back toward them. "I've been trying to deliver Marianna's answering machine for three weeks, and she's never home—not that I blame her. It's all fixed and paid for, so how about signing the receipt and saving me trip number seven?"

Frank and Joe were very happy to do that favor for her.

After the receipt was signed and the answering machine changed hands, she seemed to feel better. She drove away, giving them a wave.

"I'll bet even the CIA doesn't know about this machine," Joe said with a grin. He plugged the machine into the first outlet he found. Then he and Frank sat down on the floor to listen. Joe hit the outgoing message button first to hear Marianna's voice. She spoke in a Swedish accent: "Hello, this is Marianna. Please leave a message, and I'll call you back when it's possible."

112

"She has a nice voice—for a spy, that is," Joe said.

"What did you expect her to sound like? A character in an old spy movie?" Frank asked, pressing the button for the incoming messages.

They didn't know what to expect this time.

"Dr. Bornquist, this is Marshall at Jake's Garage. Your car will be ready at five P.M. . . . Hello, Marianna? It's me. How come you weren't at Dancercise, huh? . . . Hello, this is Bob at the tennis club. I've got to reschedule your lesson this Saturday until after my surgery. Give me a call at six six two, two nine eight nine."

There was a long silence after the last message, and Joe was about to flip the tape off. But before his hand reached the machine, another voice started talking. It was an old message, one that had been partially erased and recorded over by more recent calls, so it wasn't complete.

". . . concerned about how the plans are coming, Marianna," said a man with a British accent. His voice was friendly but sharp at the same time. "Time is running out on your father. So do send Derek some home movies to cheer him up, will you?"

It was Derek Willoughby. The answering machine had confirmed the connection once and for all. Frank and Joe felt faint chills run up and down their spines.

The tape ran on. There were other messages, and then they heard Derek Willoughby's voice once more.

113

"It's Derek again, dear. I'll be sightseeing in the States in a couple of weeks. I do hope something has *developed* by then. Where do you recommend I stay?"

Coming to the States in a few weeks. The timing was right; the accent was right. Frank and Joe were convinced that Derek Willoughby was involved in Marianna's espionage case.

"But what has this got to do with Keith?" Joe asked.

A voice answered—but it wasn't Frank's.

"Okay, you two, lie down, faces to the floor, with your hands and legs spread," a gruff voice growled behind them. "One wrong move, and I'll shoot to kill."

15 The DOTEE Factor

"Now, just who are you guys?" asked the gruff voice.

"Who wants to know?" Joe snapped.

"I've got the gun, punk," said their captor. "*I* make the rules, and *I* ask the questions. Understood?"

Frank and Joe were lying spread-eagled and facedown on the floor of the living room. They had not even seen the man's face, but they had heard him cock the hammer of his revolver. And they felt him walking closer to them. He stood over them but always cautiously out of reach of their arms.

"If you have any ID on you," he said, tapping Frank's leg with his shoe, "tell me where I can find it. If you have any weapons, you'd better tell me about those too."

"Our wallets are in our back pockets," Joe

said, lifting his head slightly to try to get a look at the man.

"I said, don't move until I tell you!" the gunman shouted.

He grabbed the wallets from their jeans pockets and was quiet for a minute. "Brothers," he murmured. "You two are a long way from home. Now sit up slowly and face me. And keep your hands flat on the floor in front of you."

Frank and Joe turned around for their first look at the man with the gun. He was muscular and solid, with the look of a retired football player. But the most surprising thing about him was the suit he was wearing—it was dark blue! Molly Frankel's prediction about a man in a dark uniform had come true.

"Do you two know how much trouble you're in?" he asked.

"Tell us," Frank said.

The man reached into his suit pocket and pulled out a photo ID.

"Phony IDs are a dime a dozen," Joe snapped.

"The only thing you have to know about this is the seal—Central Intelligence Agency," the man with the gun said. His face changed suddenly. "What are you two smiling about? I didn't tell a joke."

"CIA? Boy, are we glad to see you!" Joe said.

"Yeah, I'm sure that's what General Custer said when he saw the Indians," the CIA agent said. He leaned his face into the shade of a floor lamp that stood by a reading chair. "This is Rogers," he said. "I need a DOTEE in here."

Then he explained to Frank and Joe. "This place has more bugs in it than a flea circus," he said proudly. "The lamps, the walls, the electrical outlets, the phones. . . . We heard you come in, we heard every word you said."

Suddenly another CIA agent entered the house, carrying a portable computer. Agent Rogers handed him Frank's and Joe's IDs, and the agent immediately connected the computer to a telephone jack and began to enter information.

"This is DOTEE?" Frank asked.

"Data Over Telephone Electronics Expert," Agent Rogers said. Then he asked, "How well do you know Marianna Bornquist?"

"We *don't* know her," Frank said.

"Never met her," Joe added.

"You just work for her?" Rogers snapped.

"No, we work for her next-door neighbor," Frank said. "He's been kidnapped, and we flew to Boulder to see if his kidnapping had anything to do with the Bornquist spy case."

"Don't tell me—you're a couple of detectives." Rogers sneered.

"As a matter of fact, we are," Joe said angrily.

Agent Rogers's face tightened with impatience. "Save the fairy tales for bedtime," he snarled.

"Rogers," the DOTEE at the computer said,

"I get an affirmative on their IDs. And their father is a civilian P.I."

"Get him on the phone—now!" Rogers said.

A few calls later, Fenton Hardy answered the phone in his hotel room in Los Angeles.

"Hi, Dad," Frank said while Rogers listened carefully to every word that was said on an extension phone across the room.

"Frank," their father said cheerfully. "What did you find in Boulder?"

"A house full of CIA agents," Frank said.

Agent Rogers took over the phone then. He asked Fenton Hardy for his social security number. That was just an identification test. Then he got into details about the two Hardy boys.

Frank and Joe hung on to the phone, watching Agent Rogers's face as he listened to Fenton Hardy answer questions. And at the point when Mr. Hardy was saying that if Rogers was smart he'd bring Frank and Joe in on the investigation, Rogers exploded, "I like civilian interference about as much as I like heat rash."

"Have it your way," Fenton Hardy said. "But I don't think Carl Baumwell will like the way you're treating me and my boys."

"You know Baumwell?" Rogers asked.

"Call him and find out," Fenton Hardy said. Then he hung up.

Frank and Joe had never heard their father speak of Carl Baumwell, but the name got Agent Rogers's attention immediately.

118

Rogers ordered the DOTEE to get Carl Baumwell on the phone, which took about half an hour because he was in another country. "I didn't need trouble like this," Rogers kept telling Frank and Joe until the phone finally rang.

Whatever Carl Baumwell said to Agent Rogers completely changed the agent's attitude toward Frank and Joe.

Rogers hung up the phone and put his gun away. Then he gave Frank and Joe their wallets back. "Well, your dad knows some pretty heavy hitters in the organization," he said. "Okay, let's hear your story again. This time I'm interested."

Frank and Joe filled the CIA agent in on everything that had happened before their trip to Boulder. They told him about Marianna Bornquist's bike-riding next-door neighbor, Keith Holland, about how their case started out as harassment but had become grand larceny when the Silver Star was stolen, and finally turned into kidnapping.

"We couldn't figure out why this case kept getting bigger and bigger, until we found out about Dr. Bornquist. She's the key," Frank said.

"Why were you going crazy over her message tape?" Rogers asked.

"We'll tell you, but first tell us about her," Joe said.

"I can't," he said. "You two don't have clearance."

"We've got to find Keith, and I'm sure we can tie the kidnapping and Marianna Bornquist together," Frank said.

Rogers looked at them thoughtfully. Then he shouted at the top of his voice so that all the hidden microphones in the house could pick him up. "Get me clearance for these two from the section chief, and get it now!"

A few seconds later, the telephone in the kitchen rang. Rogers answered it. He listened for a minute, then hung up and turned back to Frank and Joe.

"Welcome to the club, boys," Rogers said with a smile.

There wasn't that much for Rogers to tell them about Marianna Bornquist. She had always been a quiet, productive, mild-mannered research scientist in a weapons lab. The government had checked her out thoroughly before giving her such a sensitive top-level job, and she was clean. She had made no political affiliations in Sweden when she was growing up, and she had made none in the States. Why she had suddenly turned traitor and photographed top-secret weapons plans was a big mystery to everyone involved.

"We found out about the microfilm and came in here with a search warrant," Rogers explained. "My men went over the house from top to bottom, but we didn't find anything. So we got a court order to impound her furniture and other personal possessions. But we didn't find

120

the microfilm in them either. Maybe she'd already passed it on to her contact."

"What's happened to her?" Joe asked.

"She was suspended from her job and went to stay with friends in Denver. But we've got our eyes on her. As soon as we can locate the microfilm, we'll arrest her. Now, what do you have for us?"

"Her accomplice," Frank said.

Agent Rogers practically fell out of his chair.

Frank and Joe played the message tape. When Derek's voice came on, they said, "That's him. His name is Derek Willoughby."

The DOTEE got busy at his computer again, calling up information on Derek Willoughby. Meanwhile, Frank and Joe told Rogers about Willoughby, his rented truck, and the last time anyone had seen the Silver Star.

"Thanks, boys," Rogers said, shaking their hands. "You've done a great service to your country."

"But you won't find Willoughby," Joe protested. "He's totally disappeared. And now it looks like he's the one who kidnapped Keith!"

"I've got a plan," Frank said.

"You boys are—as you detectives say—off the case," Rogers said.

"You don't have any idea where to look for him," stated Frank. "But I think we can make him come looking for us."

Rogers looked at Frank's face, giving him a quick lie-detector test with his eyes. What he saw was Frank's determination to find Keith Holland no matter what it took.

"Clearance!" Rogers shouted suddenly.

This time, the phone was silent.

"Come on, you guys!" he shouted again. "I don't like civilians any more than you do! But a guy's been kidnapped. If we sit here waiting for an invitation, he could get killed!"

Finally, the silence was broken when the phone rang. Rogers answered it, and this time he did more than just listen. "Oh, yeah?" he snapped. "Do you have a better plan? Because if you don't, I want clearance for these two, and I want it now!"

Rogers got what he was waiting for. Then he wrote a phone number down on his business card. "The second Willoughby makes contact, you call that number and you talk to nobody but me. Understood?"

"Understood," both brothers said.

"What's your plan?" the CIA agent wanted to know.

"I want to leave a message on Dr. Bornquist's answering machine in case Derek Willoughby calls here again," Frank said. "When he hears my voice and realizes that we can connect him with Marianna Bornquist, he'll have to come out of hiding and come after us."

It was a dangerous plan, but Rogers knew it would get quick results, so he didn't stop Frank from recording the message.

"This is Frank Hardy. Marianna can't come to

the phone right now, but if you want to talk about Keith Holland and the Silver Star, my brother and I will be back in Bayport first thing in the morning."

Rogers shook his head. His face showed his concern and doubt. "You know what you've just done, don't you?" he said. "You've just painted bright red bull's-eyes on your own backs!"

16 Riding Blind

"Frank Hardy or Joe Hardy," said a woman's friendly voice over the PA system at LaGuardia Airport, "please pick up the nearest white courtesy telephone."

Frank and Joe had just stepped off the plane in New York. They looked at each other, puzzled, wondering who was calling them. Only a few people knew they were coming in at all: their father, Agent Rogers and his CIA team, and, of course, Derek Willoughby. If he had already heard Frank's message on Marianna Bornquist's answering machine, he'd be very anxious to talk with them.

The Hardys stopped at the first white telephone they found. Frank hesitated for a second; then he lifted the receiver.

"This is Frank Hardy."

"Frank, this is Special Agent Benoir, CIA," a

man said in a businesslike voice. "I wanted you and your brother to know the good news right away. We just caught Willoughby. He surfaced about an hour ago right there at LaGuardia and our airport team nabbed him."

"That's great," Frank said. "I guess my plan worked."

"Like a charm," the CIA operative said with a chuckle. "Willoughby told us everything, but I'm afraid it's classified and not for your ears."

"That's okay, I understand," Frank said. "What about Keith Holland? Did you find him?"

"You were right about Keith, too. Willoughby kidnapped him, all right," the agent said. "Listen, I've stationed an agent there in the terminal. He'll take you to see Keith if you want to go."

"Sure, Joe and I want to see Keith," Frank said. And Joe, whose face was as happy as his brother's, nodded his head in agreement.

"Okay, here's the procedure," said Agent Benoir. "Go to luggage carousel number three. My agent will find *you*. You can't miss him. His name is Branch, and his nose looks like he ran into a brick wall—but don't say anything, because he's sensitive about it. He'll take you to Keith."

"Hey, what did old Rogers say about my plan?" Frank asked. He couldn't help gloating a little over his success.

125

"Rogers?" the agent asked. "Oh, yeah, well, you know how he is. Thanks again, guys."

Frank hung up the phone and scratched his cheek nervously. How could someone forget Rogers? But, Frank thought, the CIA *is* a big organization.

Joe slapped his brother on the back. "Wow, was that fast work or was that fast work?" he said. "They grabbed Derek Willoughby, and Keith's all right—that's what he said, isn't it?"

"Yeah," Frank said without enthusiasm.

"It's unbelievable!" Joe shouted. "Now where to?"

"The luggage claim," Frank said.

"But we don't have any bags," Joe replied.

"Someone's going to claim us," Frank said. "Come on. I'll explain on the way."

The luggage claim was on the lower level. Just about everyone stood around complaining about how badly beaten up their luggage looked after the flight. But Frank and Joe watched faces instead of luggage.

Still, they never saw the tall man who came up behind them. "Frank and Joe Hardy?" the man asked quietly.

Agent Branch's nose was everything Agent Benoir had said it was. Joe wondered whether it might have been broken by a luggage handler instead of a brick wall.

"It's a pleasure to meet you," Branch said, shaking hands with them. "We'd better get started."

"Where exactly are we going?" Joe asked.

"We shouldn't be seen talking in this crowd," the CIA agent replied briskly. "Let's just go. I've got a car waiting."

"Too fast," Frank said, shaking his head.

"How's that?" Branch asked.

"My brother thinks we're being rushed," Joe said, picking up on Frank's vibes. "Are we?"

"You're absolutely right," the agent said. "Look, I wasn't supposed to tell you this, but Keith's been hurt."

"He's what?" Frank and Joe said.

"Now maybe you understand the rush," Branch said. He put a hand on each brother's shoulder and guided them toward the door and out into the muggy New York air.

A long black limousine was parked in a no-parking zone. The driver, who was wearing a chauffeur's uniform, didn't get out to open the door when Branch brought Frank and Joe to the curb.

The brothers climbed into the backseat with the TV, the refrigerator, and the telephone. Branch sat in the front along with the chauffeur. The driver expertly maneuvered the twists and turns of the airport service roads and pulled out onto the highway. Then he did something that surprised Frank and Joe. He took off his driver's hat and loosened his tie.

"Hey, pass me up a soda. How about it?" the chauffeur called.

Frank's stomach suddenly wrapped itself in a

square knot. He recognized the chauffeur's voice! He had heard it only once, but he knew it immediately. It was the voice of Agent Benoir on the white courtesy telephone! Instantly, Frank knew that he and Joe had been led into a trap.

Frank wanted to warn Joe, without letting the two phony agents know that he was on to their secret. But Branch was watching every move they made.

"So where are we going?" Joe asked.

"Like I said, we're taking you to see Keith," Branch said.

That had sounded great in the airport. Now it made Frank feel sick.

"Yeah," Joe said in his usual persistent way, "but where are we going?"

"Just relax, Joe," Frank said, hoping his brother would get the hint. "We're going to see Keith, all right?"

Joe looked at his brother as if Frank had suddenly sprouted long furry ears. "What's wrong with you?"

"Just take it easy," Frank said, trying to say everything in those four words.

"What gives with you two?" Branch said suspiciously.

Joe wouldn't let it drop. "I just asked a simple question, that's all," he said.

The Hardy brothers froze. Suddenly, they were staring at the muzzle of a gun in Branch's hand. "Okay, just sit back, shut up, and enjoy the ride," he ordered.

"You're not CIA agents, are you?" Joe shouted.

Branch turned his head to the chauffeur, although the barrel of the gun was still pointed at Frank and Joe. "Maxie," Branch said. "Are we CIA agents? Ha ha ha! Should I break their hearts and tell them there's no Santa Claus either? Ha ha ha!"

"It's a trap! Jump!" Frank shouted to Joe. Even though the car was speeding down the highway, Frank grabbed for the door handle and yanked it hard—but the doors had been locked electronically.

Both men in the front seat had a good laugh. Then Maxie, the chauffeur, spoke up again, looking at Frank and Joe in the rearview mirror. "You know, Branch," he said, "I think I'm going to like working with kids. They're so easy to fool."

"What are you guys going to do with us?" Frank asked.

"Anything Derek Willoughby tells us to do," Branch said.

Willoughby again!

"Wait a minute," Frank said. "You mean Willoughby set up this trap? How did he find out we talked to the CIA? That was just a few hours ago!"

Branch laughed. "Willoughby has friends all over," he said. "I think you met his good friend Buck, the cowboy cabbie."

Branch laughed at the look on Frank's face.

129

"We've been on your tail forever," he said. "Get the picture? Now enjoy it in silence."

After a few tense, quiet miles, Maxie checked his watch and said, "It's time, Branch."

He steered the car off the highway and onto the shoulder. When the car stopped, Branch cocked his gun and said, "Don't move."

Frank and Joe held still while Maxie got into the backseat and tied Frank's hands behind him. Then he put a blindfold around Frank's eyes. Next it was Joe's turn to be tied and blindfolded.

"You're lower than slime," Joe muttered. Maxie didn't reply; he merely shoved Joe back into the limousine.

The car started up again with Frank and Joe helpless and blind in the backseat. It was much worse this way, and both brothers wished they had kept their mouths shut a little longer.

After driving for some time—it was hard to tell how long—Frank and Joe heard the road change from pavement to gravel. A few miles later, the car stopped. Nothing happened for a few awful moments while the brothers sweated it out. The silence and blind waiting were unbearable. They couldn't even hear Branch or Maxie talking, because Maxie had closed the glass window between the front and back seats.

Finally, the back door opened. Frank and Joe could hear a train whistle somewhere in the distance.

"Get out," Branch said. "We're changing to another car."

Joe was the first to slide toward the door, but, instead of climbing out of the car, he pretended to stumble and fall headfirst. He hit the ground, and with his hands tied behind his back he flopped around like a hooked fish.

But he got what he wanted. His blindfold lifted from one of his eyes. And for a few seconds, he saw that they were parked in a wooded area. A train station was across the road, a small station surrounded by trees. It looked like rural Connecticut, which would mean they were an hour or two away from New York. He squirmed and tried to see more, but Maxie pulled him to his feet.

"His blindfold's come loose," Maxie said, pulling the cloth back over Joe's eyes.

"You know what that means, don't you?" Branch said menacingly.

"I didn't see anything," Joe tried to explain.

"Willoughby won't take that chance," Branch said. "Now you won't leave here alive, kid."

Branch pushed Joe forward, opened a different car door, and forced Joe into the smaller backseat.

"You're next," Branch said, grabbing Frank out of the limo by the lapels of the light summer jacket he wore.

Suddenly Branch yanked Frank violently out of the car and onto the ground.

"What the blazes is this?" Branch shouted.

From inside the dark blindfold, Frank didn't

131

know what Branch was talking about. "It's my jacket," Frank said.

"Keep your voice down," Maxie cautioned.

Branch snapped back at his partner, "Oh yeah? Look what I found under his jacket collar, and then tell me to keep my voice down."

"A homing device?" Maxie said.

Frank had no idea how it had gotten there, but he figured that Agent Rogers must have slipped it on him sometime in Boulder. Suddenly he was glad that Rogers was a man who didn't like to take chances.

"You know what that means, don't you?" Frank said, suddenly taunting Branch with his own words. "It means the CIA has been following us the whole time. They know exactly where we are. You'd better give up."

Crunch! Maxie stepped on the electronic device. "Let's go before the government guys come crawling all over us like ants at a picnic," he said.

Branch quickly searched Joe, but there wasn't another device.

"Now I'll tell you what that homing device *really* means," Branch said. His voice sounded edged with panic. "It means *both* of you don't have as long to live as you thought!"

17 Derek Willoughby

"Come on, Branch, let's get out of here," Maxie said. "Who knows how close the feds are?"

Branch roughly pushed Frank into the backseat of the second car. It was much smaller and smelled awful. Then Maxie sped off.

"This thing can't hold the road like the limo did," Maxie commented when the tires squealed coming out of a sharp curve.

"Then why don't you slow down?" Joe shouted.

Just for that, Maxie sped up. Frank and Joe were still tied and blindfolded, so they couldn't see the road ahead and had no way of bracing themselves when the car took a sudden turn. They bounced around the backseat like pinballs until their shoulders hurt from hitting the doors.

About five minutes and seven turns later,

133

without a warning, Maxie hit the brakes hard, and the car skidded to a stop. Frank and Joe didn't need to see in order to know that they had arrived at their final destination.

"I'm going in to tell him about the homing device," Branch said. "He may just want to rabbit out of here."

Branch got out of the car. While he was gone, Maxie untied the blindfolds. Suddenly Frank noticed Maxie's hands.

"Hey, did you lose a driving glove?" he asked.

"Yeah. How'd you know?" Maxie answered.

"Because I think I found it."

Maxie glared at Frank. "How could *you* find it? It's been missing for four days," he said.

Before Frank could answer, Branch was back, dragging Frank and Joe from the backseat and pushing them into a small, simple cabin with woods visible from every window.

Keith Holland sat tied to a chair in the corner. On the floor in front of him lay the shiny Silver Star—completely disassembled. The handlebars were by the bed, the frame was next to the dresser, the wheels were both off, and the seat lay at Keith's feet.

Sitting at a small table in the middle of the room was the man the Hardy boys had been looking for, Derek Willoughby. They recognized him immediately as the face on the passport in the Easy-Haul office.

"Welcome, chaps," Derek said. His voice was much friendlier than his face. "I understand we don't have as much time as I'd hoped, thanks to Branch and Maxie's incompetence in not finding the homing device you were wearing. They should have searched you straight away. But they're Yanks, and you Yanks are such a sloppy bunch."

"Oh yeah? We caught on to you, didn't we?" Joe said bitterly.

Derek Willoughby let out a long breath. "I must say, you two are a pair," he said with a smile. "I have outwitted the intelligence forces of more nations than I can count. To be snagged by a couple of teenagers is almost embarrassing."

Frank didn't want to hear any more boasting from the spy, so he turned his attention to Keith. Keith sat motionless and silent, although he wasn't gagged. He was tied to a straight-backed wooden chair. Frank and Joe could see on his face that he had been through the worst forty-eight hours of his life.

"Are you all right?" Frank asked.

"Keith has been instructed to keep his mouth shut unless he has something he wishes to tell me and *only* me," Derek said. "And Keith knows what that is, don't you, my boy?" He turned to Frank and Joe. "And now it's your turn to talk, chaps. I got your message on Marianna's machine. Tell me quickly now, where is the microfilm?"

"Uh, it's exactly where it's supposed to be," Frank said. He was stalling, trying to fool Willoughby into giving out more information than he was getting.

"No, it's not, as you can plainly see," Willoughby said.

Frank and Joe scanned the small cabin again. Everything in it was ordinary except for the disassembled bicycle and the kidnapped cyclist.

"What's the matter—didn't Marianna Bornquist give you good advice about sightseeing?" Joe said.

Willoughby's face went white. "So that's how you two found me out," he said. "Those telephone answering machines are more trouble than they're worth."

"And Marianna told us the rest, all of it," Joe said.

"Alas, Marianna is a dear girl, but she was never cut out for a business like this," Willoughby said. "I mean, really—running over to the next-door neighbor's garage and stuffing top-secret microfilm into the frame of a bicycle—strictly amateurish."

"She was under a lot of pressure," Frank said.

"Yes, I know," Derek Willoughby said with a sigh. "Your CIA operatives were breathing down her neck. But when she told me what she had done, I could have killed her."

The words sent a shudder through Frank and Joe.

"She was so proud of herself when she called, I had to laugh," Willoughby said, laughing now. "She said she had put the microfilm in a perfectly safe place and she just knew it would be easy for me to get it."

"So you came to America to steal the Silver Star because Marianna said she put the microfilm in it," Frank said. He gestured toward Maxie and Branch. "But why did you hire these two goons?"

"I prefer to work alone, it's true. But I needed someone to help me," Willoughby said. "There were so many people interfering with my plans, present company included."

"But you had the bike. Why did you kidnap Keith?" Joe asked.

Willoughby was on his feet now, pacing back and forth across the floor. "Well, imagine my surprise after I took the bike apart piece by piece and discovered the microfilm wasn't in it. That's when I decided Keith Holland had found it first."

Willoughby moved back to the kitchen table. He poured tea with one hand and milk with the other into a cup. Then he took a sip before continuing his story. "It actually kept me awake nights, wondering whether this young man who had *my* microfilm was trying to be a hero with it or was trying to make some money by selling it on the black market."

Keith suddenly spoke up. "I've told you a million times I don't know where it is," he said.

Willoughby ran over and slapped Keith's face with the back of his hand. "Shut up!" he shouted. "I said *only* if you told me exactly

137

where the microfilm was, *then* I'd let you live a little longer, remember?"

Keith was breathing hard, and Branch moved over toward Willoughby. "You didn't say anything about really killing anyone," Branch said.

"Don't stick your nose where it doesn't belong," Willoughby said contemptuously.

"Don't make jokes about my nose," Branch said.

"Just shut up, everyone, while I think. There may not be much time left," Willoughby said. He walked away from Keith and paced again.

In the silence that followed, Frank realized what they were up against. Willoughby was a madman who wouldn't hesitate to kill. And the only reason he hadn't done so yet was that he believed Keith, Frank, and Joe really knew where the microfilm was. So Frank took a deep breath and played his highest card.

"Willoughby, I'll tell you where the microfilm is," Frank said.

Even the dust stopped moving in the cabin—but then Joe stirred it up again by flying into a sudden rage. "What do you think you're doing?" he shouted angrily.

Frank knew immediately that his brother had seen the game and was ready to join in. But he was almost afraid to look at Willoughby's face to see if he bought it too. And, more important, he had to be sure that Keith understood that it was all a charade. Otherwise, Keith could blow the whole thing.

"Untie him," Willoughby ordered Branch. The tall man quickly obeyed his boss. Frank stood up and rubbed his wrist. Then he walked over to face Keith. "I'm going to tell them, and I don't care how much you yell about it," Frank said.

From the back, Willoughby and the others saw Frank standing over Keith, threatening the tied-up bike rider. Only Keith could see the quick wink of Frank's right eye.

Frank turned back to Willoughby and said, "I'll tell you, but we've got to have some assurances that you won't kill us as soon as you have the microfilm."

"I just want the microfilm," Willoughby said calmly. "That's all I am being paid to do. Everybody walks once I have it. You have my word."

"Okay," Frank said. "It's in a secret compartment in the bike. But you've got to put the bike together to find it."

"Now I think you're pulling my leg," Willoughby said with a smile.

"Frank, you traitor!" Keith shouted, playing along beautifully with Frank and Joe's charade.

"Listen, you hired us to save your skin, and that's what we're doing. We wouldn't even be here now if it weren't for you, Keith. So shut up!" Frank wheeled around and faced his brother. "You have something to say about it?"

Joe said nothing. So Frank walked over to the spread-out pieces of the Silver Star.

"The microfilm is in a special spring-loaded compartment," Frank said. "It'll only open with the full weight of a rider in the seat."

"I've never heard of anything like that," Willoughby said.

Of course you haven't, Frank thought, because it doesn't exist. But I'd better think of a way to convince you that it does—or my plan will never work.

18 Race Against Time

"Of course you've never heard of anything like that," Frank said out loud. He tried to sound confident. "That's because there's never been a bicycle like the Silver Star before."

Willoughby smiled sarcastically. "You mean the bicycle was designed to carry microfilm?" he asked.

"No," Frank said. "It was designed to carry salt and sugar tablets right at the racer's fingertips. Everything about this bike is based on weight and leverage and angles."

Willoughby didn't move. He had one of those faces that never show any emotion. You could never be certain of what he was thinking. But he made up his mind quickly. He pointed to Maxie and Branch and said, "Put the bike back together."

Maxie didn't look pleased, but he got to work.

141

"Care for some tea while we're waiting?" Willoughby asked Frank and Joe.

"I could use something to eat," Joe said. "And I'd be happy to clean out your refrigerator for you, if you'd untie me."

Willoughby nodded and motioned to Frank to untie his brother.

"Great," said Joe, standing up and flexing his hands. "Now, where's the food?"

Nobody could play a meatball teenager better than Joe—except Chet Morton, whom Joe was imitating. It was a favorite disguise. He'd move into a kitchen and act like a human vacuum cleaner, but his eyes secretly checked out every possible escape plan. And this time they were going to need one in a hurry.

"Well, tell me, how was Callie's party?" Willoughby asked.

Frank and Joe hated him for invading their personal lives. He went on, "You worried so much about what to wear to the party I wondered if you ever got there at all."

He was letting the Hardy brothers know that it was he who had planted the bug in their van and that he knew things about them.

So Frank played the same game, showing Willoughby that they had figured things out about him, too. "You spoiled the party by wrecking Keith's camper," Frank said. "We had to leave early."

"Before they cut the cake, too," Joe called with his head in the refrigerator. By this time he

142

had eliminated the windows as an escape route because their screens were new and tightly nailed in. There was no back door.

"That's a shame," Willoughby said with a laugh. "Do hurry with the bicycle, chaps. I'm most eager to see it demonstrated."

Maxie looked up from the bicycle parts that surrounded him on the floor. "Anytime you want to take over, just say the word," he invited Willoughby.

"Why are Americans so cranky?" Willoughby said.

"Why don't you let me help?" Keith suggested.

"Because that would involve untying you," Willoughby said.

"Sorry," Keith said. "I thought you were in a hurry."

"All right. Untie him, Branch."

Keith joined Branch and Maxie on the floor and sped up the assembly of the Silver Star.

Joe was still in the kitchen, and when Willoughby wasn't watching he quietly opened and closed, opened and closed, opened and closed the refrigerator door for his brother's benefit.

Frank got the message. They would have to escape through the front door. Frank mentally filed the message away for later use.

A little while later, the Silver Star stood gleaming, proud, and whole once again. Willoughby circled it, motioning for everyone but Frank to stand away.

143

Willoughby smiled. "It really is a marvelous piece of work, isn't it?" he said.

"You haven't seen anything yet," Frank said, preparing to mount the bike.

"Well, do show me, dear boy," Willoughby said.

"Glad to," said Frank.

"Now!" shouted Joe.

Everything happened at once. Frank hopped on the Silver Star and began pedaling like crazy. Joe launched himself into the air, aiming his shoulder directly at Willoughby's stomach. Willoughby hit the ground like a used tea bag. Keith leaped for the front door and opened it just in time for Frank to go sailing through on the bike. Then Keith threw a chair at Maxie and Branch.

"You fools!" Frank could hear Derek Willoughby shouting, but his voice was already fading as Frank rode away.

The bike moved gracefully, effortlessly, as Frank's legs pumped. He was riding down the curved, hilly dirt road that had brought them up to the cabin. He pumped a little harder, knowing that Willoughby, Maxie, and Branch would start following him as soon as they could jump into a car.

Joe and Keith would keep them busy as long as they could. But soon, it would be just him, the road, and the bike versus three armed and dangerous men in a car.

"Don't think about anything except your

144

legs," Frank muttered, remembering what Keith had said. That helped Frank forget about the life-and-death race he was running and helped him concentrate on his riding.

He was down the hill and onto the main road, hoping it would take him back to the little town where he had heard the train. He also hoped the CIA had followed the homing device at least that far.

Hoooonnnnnnk! A car horn blasted in the distance behind him. Willoughby was coming for him! Frank's legs had stopped aching already, and now they were growing numb, but his fierce concentration kept them pumping at a steady pace.

The car horn was getting closer. Ahead, Frank saw some parked cars along the road. But the closer he got to them, the more he realized that they weren't parked *along* the road at all. They were parked *across* the road. It was a roadblock!

Frank pedaled faster and faster in rhythm with his heartbeat. He couldn't breathe, but he knew that if he made it to the roadblock he would be safe.

The cars separated just in time for Frank to pass through, and then they closed the road again instantly. Men with automatic revolvers leaped from behind the cars. Every gun was pointed at the little car that came roaring down behind Frank.

The car screeched to a swerving stop before it reached the roadblock. For a single tense moment, Frank waited for the awful sound of gunfire, but it never came. Instead, Frank saw Maxie and Branch throw their guns through the windows onto the ground. Then they climbed quickly out of the little car with their hands high in the air, telling anyone who would listen that they surrendered.

Then Derek Willoughby, complete with black eye, stepped out of the car with his hands up too—followed by Joe Hardy and Keith Holland, who came running over to find Frank. He was sitting exhausted on the ground.

"Frank," Keith said, putting his hand on the tired Hardy brother's shoulder, "if you ever give up being a detective, consider a career as a racer. That was *great* riding."

"You guys were great," Frank said. "You gave me the time I needed."

"It was a pleasure flattening Willoughby," Joe said. "Anytime."

"I loved the bit about the secret compartment in the bike and putting your weight on the seat," Keith said. "How did you ever come up with that?"

"I had to think of some way to get them to put the bike back together, or I knew we'd never get out of there," Frank said. "And you guys played it beautifully."

Just then the three of them were joined by Agent Rogers, who had been there at the road-block directing the operation. "Sorry to break

146

up this mutual admiration society," he said, "but I've got some questions."

"First, aren't you dying to tell us what a brilliant plan it was?" Joe said.

"It could have been a lot better if you had kept the homing device secured," Agent Rogers said.

"That would have been easier if you had told us about it in the first place," Frank scolded.

"Must have slipped my mind," Agent Rogers said with a cough. "Where's the microfilm?"

"It's in Keith's bike, just where Marianna Bornquist put it," Frank said.

"Come on," Agent Rogers said. "Willoughby must have gone over every inch of the Silver Star."

"He did," Frank said. "But that's not the bike I'm talking about. The way I figure it, Marianna Bornquist panicked when she knew you CIA types were on the way to her house. So she ran next door and put the microfilm in Keith's bike. She knew Keith was leaving the next day for a big race of some kind on the Silver Star—and she told that to Willoughby."

"But I was already gone," Keith put in. "I was in Los Angeles in Michael Saperstein's development laboratory."

Joe's eyes brightened. "I get it! Saperstein would never let you keep a ten-thousand-dollar prototype bike in your garage," he said.

"That's right, Joe," Keith said. He turned to

147

Frank. "The bike you're talking about is a beautiful silver job—but it's not the Silver Star. The Silver Star has never seen the inside of my garage."

Agent Rogers burst out laughing. "Hey, Willoughby!" he shouted to Derek Willoughby, who was under armed guard in one of the CIA's cars. "You hear this? The film is still in a bicycle in Keith Holland's garage!"

Willoughby's face fell. "You teenagers have completely ruined my credibility," he said.

"Well, Keith, you'll be glad to hear my news, too," Rogers said. "We finally had a long talk with Marianna Bornquist. And we found out why she agreed to work with Willoughby. It was because of her father."

"Marianna and her father were very close." Keith nodded. "She liked to talk to me about what a wonderful man he was. He never came over to America. She only saw him when she went back home to Sweden. But about a year ago, he disappeared in a skiing accident and was presumed dead, although his body was never found. I don't think Marianna entirely snapped out of that shock."

"And that's exactly what Willoughby was counting on," Rogers said.

"A month or so ago, he contacted Marianna with some surprising news. Willoughby told her that her father wasn't dead after all. He said he was alive but had been kidnapped and was being held prisoner by a foreign country, a foreign country that just happened to know that Marianna Bornquist had access to U.S. military secrets."

"I get it," Frank said. "Willoughby probably told her this country would trade her father for weapons designs."

"Right," the CIA agent said. "Of course, none of it was true. Willoughby was just using her to get what he wanted."

Keith shook his head sadly. "I know Marianna would do anything to bring her father back to life—even something she knew was totally wrong," he said.

"Willoughby passed himself off as the middleman," Rogers said. "He pretended to be acting in her best interests. The truth is, Willoughby is a British agent who went into business for himself, selling top-secret information to the highest bidder. We don't know who he was supposed to trade with this time, but, because of you three, he won't be trading with anyone ever again."

The boys were quiet after Rogers finished. "Poor Marianna," Keith said. "I'll bet she could use a friend right now."

"Well, that's it," Rogers said. "We're going to have to impound your bike in Boulder, Keith, for the microfilm."

"If you don't get it, rust will," Keith said with a smile. "I'm never going to ride another bike."

"What?" Frank and Joe shouted.

"Right," Agent Rogers said. "Well, let's endeavor to keep out of each other's way in the

149

future." Rogers growled the words, but he shook hands with Keith, Joe, and Frank before he walked away.

"What did you mean, you're never going to ride another bike?" Joe said.

"I meant I'll never ride a bike that isn't the Silver Star," Keith said, laughing. "And thanks to you guys, I've got the one and only Silver Star in my hands again. You never quit on me, and that was just the kind of support team I needed. I'm really grateful."

"It's just a shame that you and the Silver Star couldn't finish Bike-Aid," Frank said. "I'll bet Gregg Angelotti has crossed the finish line by now."

"You're probably right about Gregg, but who said I'm not going to finish the race?" Keith asked.

"Molly Frankel did," Joe reminded him.

"Well, this time she was wrong," Keith said. "I always finish what I start. Every mile I ride means more money for poor people. That's what it says in my contract, and that's what I'm going to do."

"I guess Molly owes you an apology," Frank said. Then he covered his eyes with his hand. "Wait. . . . I'm getting a vision. . . . I see Molly What's-her-face. . . . She's standing in front of a lot of microphones. And she's apologizing for accepting Dave Luckey's bribe to say bummer things about Keith Holland!"

"All right!" Joe said.

"We'll see if we can make that vision come true as soon as we get back to Bayport," Frank added.

"What's your hurry?" Keith asked. "I hear Maine is beautiful this time of year. Why don't you come along with me?"

"That sounds great!" Joe said.

"But I think we'll take our van," Frank said. "I do my best cycling only when there are bad guys following me!"

Keith climbed onto the Silver Star and did a smooth, slow wheelie.

"Hope I didn't do anything to wreck the bike," Frank said, remembering his rough-and-tumble ride down the hill.

"Are you kidding?" Keith said with a smile. "This bike is indestructible. Besides, you guys got the Silver Star back on its wheels. And when it goes into production, I'm going to make sure you get the first two bikes that come off the line!"

Frank and Joe just smiled at each other.

"So let's get out of here," Keith added. "The finish line is waiting—and I'm already late!"